TM

Silhouette

D0051604

Be My Baby

HOLLY JACOBS

SILHOUETTE

Romance®

$4.25 U.S.
$4.99 CAN.

INTIMATE MOMENTS™

From *New York Times* Bestselling Author

HEATHER GRAHAM
IN THE DARK

(Silhouette Intimate Moments #1309)

After she'd stumbled onto the body of a dead woman,
Alexandra McCord's working paradise had turned into a
nightmare. With a hurricane raging, Alex was stranded with her
ex-husband, David Denham—the man she'd never forgotten.
And even though his sudden return cast doubt on his motives,
Alex had no choice but to trust in the safety of his embrace.
Because a murderer was walking among them and no matter
what, she knew her heart—or her life—would be forfeit.

ISBN 0-373-19733-0

9 780373 197330

50425

EAN

Available at your favorite retail outlet.

"Amelia, thank God you're still here," Mac called.

"What did you need," she said.

"I need you," he replied.

Mia managed to keep from choking at his reply. "Pardon me?"

"Not *you*, your help," he corrected himself. "Get in the car, please?"

"But—"

"*Please*, Amelia?"

There was something in his voice that told Mia that now was not the time to argue or taunt him. Something was wrong. She waddled her well-layered self toward the car, and as she got closer she heard noise. Lots of noise. It wasn't music. Or if it was, it was the most awful music ever.

It sounded like—

A baby.

A crying baby.

Larry Mackenzie had a crying baby in his back seat.

* * *

Dear Reader,

Whether our heroes are flirting with their best friends or taking care of adorable tots, their stories of falling for the right woman are sure to melt your heart. Don't miss one magical moment of this month's collection from Silhouette Romance.

Carolyn Zane begins THE BRUBAKER BRIDES miniseries by introducing us to the first of three Texas-bred sisters, in *Virginia's Getting Hitched* (SR #1730). Dr. Virginia Brubaker knows the secret to a long-lasting relationship: compatibility. But one sexy, irreverent ranch hand has a different theory all together…that he hopes to test on the prim but not-so-proper doctor!

In *Just Between Friends* (SR #1731), the latest emotion-packed tale from Julianna Morris, a handsome contractor rescues his well-to-do best friend by agreeing to marry her—for a year. But he doesn't know about her little white lie—for them, she's always wanted more than friendship….

Prince Perfect always answers the call of duty…to his sons and to his kingdom. But his beautiful nanny tempts him to let go of his inhibitions and give in to the call of the heart. Find out if this bachelor dad will make the perfect husband, in *Falling for Prince Federico* (SR #1732) by Nicole Burnham.

The newest title from Holly Jacobs, *Be My Baby* (SR #1733), promises a rollicking good time! When a carefree single guy finds a baby on his doorstep, he's sure things couldn't get worse—until he's stranded in a snowstorm with his annoyingly attractive receptionist. With sparks flying, they're guaranteed to stay warm!

Sincerely,

Mavis C. Allen
Associate Senior Editor

Please address questions and book requests to:
Silhouette Reader Service
U.S.: 3010 Walden Ave., P.O. Box 1325, Buffalo, NY 14269
Canadian: P.O. Box 609, Fort Erie, Ont. L2A 5X3

Be My Baby

HOLLY JACOBS

SILHOUETTE *Romance* ®

Published by Silhouette Books

America's Publisher of Contemporary Romance

This one is for Larry who, although we've never met,
has great taste in taco joints and in sisters! It's also for
Allison, with many thanks for everything—it was a joy
working with you. Finally for Rachel,
who doesn't pop her gum, but does great nails!

 SILHOUETTE BOOKS

ISBN 0-373-19733-0

BE MY BABY

Copyright © 2004 by Holly Fuhrmann

This edition published by arrangement with Harlequin Books S.A.

® and TM are trademarks of Harlequin Books S.A., used under license.
Trademarks indicated with ® are registered in the United States Patent
and Trademark Office, the Canadian Trade Marks Office and in other
countries.

Visit Silhouette Books at www.eHarlequin.com

Printed in U.S.A.

Books by Holly Jacobs

Silhouette Romance

Do You Hear What I Hear? #1557
A Day Late and a Bride Short #1653
Dad Today, Groom Tomorrow #1683
Be My Baby #1733

*Perry Square

HOLLY JACOBS

can't remember a time when she didn't read…and read a lot. Writing her own stories just seemed a natural outgrowth of that love. Reading, writing, chauffeuring kids to and from activities makes for a busy life. But it's one she wouldn't trade for any other.

Holly lives in Erie, Pennsylvania, with her husband, four children and a one-hundred-and-eighty-pound Old English mastiff. In her "spare" time, Holly loves hearing from her fans. You can write to her at P.O. Box 11102, Erie, PA 16514-1102 or visit her Web site at www.HollysBooks.com.

Lake Erie (5 blocks North)

Snips and Snaps

Wagner, Chambers, McDuffy and Donovan Law Firm

Gardner Ophthamology

By Design

The Chocolate Bar

North Park Row

West Perry Square

East Perry Square

Peach St.

State St.

French St.

Mabel's Acupuncture

N

Police Station

Five and Dime

South Park Row

Erie, PA
Perry Square

Chapter One

"The forecast for Erie, Pennsylvania, calls for lake-effect snow. We're expecting anywhere from twelve to more than eighteen inches in the snowbelt tonight. Just another snowy Erie winter. It's good to know that some things never change…"

Change.

Amelia Gallagher switched off the radio with a bit more force than was required. She could do with a change. But it looked like what she was getting was more snow.

A lot more snow.

"If you keep glaring like that, you're going to scare away the paying customers," Larry Mackenzie said as he walked into Wagner, McDuffy, Chambers and Donovan law firm.

She watched him as he stomped his feet on the entryway floor, leaving a small pile of snow on the carpet.

Mac was easy on the eyes. As a matter of fact, some might say the phrase tall, dark and handsome had been invented with him in mind. But Amelia knew the truth. Her mother used to say *pretty is as pretty does,* and what Larry Mackenzie did best was annoy her.

Of course, she did her best to annoy him right back.

He didn't feel the name *Larry* inspired the type of confidence an attorney should inspire, so he preferred being called Mac, which is precisely why Amelia said, *"Larry—"*

"Mac," he corrected her for the millionth time.

Amelia hid a smile as she continued. "You're making a mess on the floor and I'm not cleaning it up."

He scowled, which cheered her considerably.

She handed him a number of memos. "You've had three messages from a Kim Lindsay while you were at court. She says to call her right away."

He glanced at the top paper she handed him and studied the name a moment. "Lindsay…Kim Lindsay? It doesn't ring a bell. Did she say what it was about?"

Amelia shrugged. "Listen, I just take the messages, I don't get an autobiography. You probably met her at a bar last week and have forgotten her already."

"The only bar I attended was a *Bar* Mitzvah for Mark's kid."

"Funny, Larry."

That was the thing about Larry Mackenzie—he thought he was funny.

Come to think of it, most people agreed with him. But Amelia didn't, although she could think of a number of descriptions she did feel suited him.

Annoying.

Egotistical.

Frustrating.

Cavalier.

Annoying…oh, she'd already thought that.

Gorgeous, if a woman was into superficial looks… which Amelia wasn't. It's just sometimes she forgot she wasn't and couldn't help but enjoy the view.

Like right now, as he stood, laughing because he thought he'd verbally bested her with his *Bar Mitzvah* comment…if he was anyone else, she'd have to say that twinkle of humor in his eye was endearing.

But endearing wasn't one of the words she'd ever use to describe Larry Mackenzie.

To clear her head of such inappropriate thoughts, she stared at the puddle he left on the floor with his unstomped shoes.

There. She felt better.

Larry was annoying.

Egotistical.

She sighed as she realized that she was just re-cycling terms. She'd just have to spend the rest of her day thinking up other appropriate adjectives—non-gorgeous ones—to describe Larry Mackenzie. It wouldn't do to run out of them if she needed them.

"Listen, if you can't manage calling me Mac, maybe you should call me Mr. Mackenzie?"

"Or maybe I should simply call you—"

She couldn't think of a barb to end the sentence with, but thankfully, Larry would never know be-cause at the moment, Elias Donovan, the firm's new-est partner, walked into the building and said, "Tsk, tsk, tsk, kids. If you're going to fight, I'm going to have to put you in separate corners."

He'd kicked off most of the snow outside on the steps, which was considerate, unlike some people who didn't care how much work they made for others.

"Separate is always good, at least when it comes to *Larry* and me," she said.

Mac, without saying another word, stalked up the stairs toward his office.

"Do you have to pick on him like that?" Dono-van asked.

"No. I also don't *have* to floss every day, but I like

my teeth and hope to keep them, so I do. Just like I enjoy needling Mac and would hate to lose my edge."

Donovan laughed as he started up the stairs to his office. He turned and added, "In case I forget later, call me if you need a ride Monday, okay? Your car won't make it out of the drive if the storm hits."

"Thanks, Donovan," Amelia said.

Donovan was a nice guy…unlike some other people in this firm.

Why, Mac wouldn't care if she got stuck somewhere between home and work, but Donovan did. He'd just purchased a new four-wheel-drive truck last fall and had given her rides on a few of the worst days between then and now.

Of course, it helped that she was good friends with his wife, Sarah. Sarah worried about her and probably told Donovan to ask. But it didn't matter who told him, Donovan was a nice guy who was right, her car wouldn't make it if the storm hit.

Amelia's old car was on its last legs—or tires as the case may be. But she'd just paid her brother's last tuition payment, and as soon as she could save up a down payment, she was going to celebrate by buying a new car.

Brand new.

Something that had that new car smell.

Cloth seats at the very least.

Maybe even leather.

Her friend, Libby, had just bought a new car with automatic ignition and electric seat-warmers. Just push a little button from the warmth of your house, and then walk out five minutes later to a warm car and warm seats.

Oh, the utter decadent luxury of it all.

Soon Amelia would save enough money to get something like it. After years of taking care of other people, she would finally be able to concentrate on what she wanted.

Their dad had left them when Amelia was young, not that he'd ever really been with them, even when he still lived at home.

She hadn't mourned her father's leaving. But her mom…when she had died, Amelia thought her heart would break. She was only twenty-one, but knew what she had to do. She dropped out of college and took over as head of the family. Her brothers deserved all the breaks she could give them.

After scrimping and scraping for the last six years to get both Marty and Ryan through college, she was now a financially independent woman. She'd spent her life looking after people, now all she had to do was look after herself. She could do all the things she'd always dreamed of.

At least, she could if she could figure them out.

Maybe she'd go back to school. Maybe she'd take up skydiving. Maybe…

There was a world of opportunity out there. A new car with seat-warmers was just the start. Life was just waiting for Amelia Gallagher to discover it.

No, not Amelia.

That was a name that sounded weighted with responsibilities.

Mia.

Her family had always called her Mia when she was younger. When she was carefree. Somewhere along the line they'd stopped and she'd become Amelia.

Amelia. The responsible one. The one who took care of things…who took care of the rest of them.

Well, she was carefree again and she would soon discover what that meant. She was Mia again. Amelia might not know just what she was going to do, but Mia was going to figure it out.

Annoying attorneys forgotten, Mia continued to fantasize about all the things she could do now, starting with the car she was going to buy soon.

Very soon.

"This is just a stop-gap measure, Mr. Mackenzie. You'll have to decide soon, very soon."

"Legally, it's my right." Mac didn't know many things—and at this moment, the biggest thing he didn't know was what he was doing—but he knew the law.

"I don't know if exercising that right is in the best

interest of the child, and that's all that concerns me," Ms. Lindsay said, giving him a look that clearly stated that she was positive Mac couldn't handle the job.

"Her mother named me guardian, and as such, it's up to me to worry about Katie's upbringing."

He was responsible. The thought scared Mac to the very core of his being, and he was man enough to admit it. At least to himself.

He was responsible for a baby.

He wasn't sure what he was going to do about her, but he was sure he wouldn't drop the ball…not like his parents had.

He slammed the door shut on that thought.

He wouldn't mess things up for this baby like his parents messed things up for him.

It wasn't as if it was a life-long commitment. He would find her a home—a loving, dependable adoptive home with people who would love her and always be there for her—and that would be that.

It amazed him how much things had changed in just one short hour.

Just sixty minutes ago he'd returned Kim Lindsay's call. Of all the things he'd expected, this wasn't even the glimmer of a possibility. And yet, here he was, standing in the middle of Esther Thomas's living room with the mysterious Kim Lindsay.

She wasn't someone he'd met and forgotten as Amelia had suggested. Leave it to Amelia to always suspect the worst of him. Just this once, he wished she'd been right. It would be so much easier if Kim Lindsay was just another person he'd met and could forget. But no, Ms. Lindsay was a social worker assigned to his case.

Not his case, but Katie O'Keefe's case. It had been Kim Lindsay's job to find out if the infant had any relatives to care for her and to make arrangements if she didn't.

Katie O'Keefe didn't have any relatives, but she had Mac.

Her guardian.

He was responsible for the baby. That was something Ms. Lindsay was having problems remembering.

"I already have a foster home lined up for her," Ms. Lindsay said. "The super let me into Marion's apartment and I found your name as her emergency contact."

"Not an emergency contact, a guardian. I've shown you copies of all the papers." He was glad that he'd thought to bring them.

"And you told me that you never imagined it would come to this, that you don't know the first thing about babies, and don't plan on keeping her. If that's the case—"

"I'd be willing to keep her, for a fee. Just enough to cover the costs," Esther Thomas wheedled.

Mac looked at Marion O'Keefe's neighbor. She

looked frail with age, hardly able to take care of herself, much less a baby.

"No," he said, his response was quickly echoed by the social worker. They exchanged conspiratorial smiles. They might not agree on where Katie O'Keefe should stay, but they obviously had no trouble agreeing it wasn't here.

"I mean," Mac said when the old woman scowled, "while I appreciate all you've done for Katie, her mother wanted me to care for her, and that's just what I'm going to do."

"Ms. Thomas, would you excuse us a moment?" Ms. Lindsay asked.

"Yeah, whatever. Her mother never wanted me to baby-sit either, as if I can't take care of a baby…" The older woman wandered down the hall, muttering to herself.

Ms. Lindsay studied a file.

Mac recognized the move. He often employed it himself. Looking at the file gave her a feeling of authority, reminding both of them that she was in charge.

Mac waited to see what her next argument was.

He didn't have to wait long.

She looked up from the chart and met his gaze. Before she could say anything he said, "I'm taking her with me. After all, it's just short-term. Her mother trusted me with her care."

"Tell me again how that came about?"

"Ms. O'Keefe didn't have any family. The baby's father died before she was born. Marion wanted to see to it her daughter never ended up in a foster home. She knew she needed a guardian, someone to see to the baby's future in case anything happened. She'd read about some of my cases, and knew that I'd been instrumental in arranging a few adoptions."

Mac did pro-bono work for Our Home, a nonprofit agency that tried to place special needs children into adoptive families. But he didn't work with the children personally and he'd never served as anyone's guardian.

He should have told the woman no. It was legal in Pennsylvania for a lawyer to serve as guardian, but rare. He should have simply said no.

Mac had been ready to do just that. But when Marion O'Keefe had come to his office she'd seemed so alone as she told him her story. And despite his best intentions, he empathized. He knew what that felt like to have no one to turn to.

She'd looked at him, her need apparent in her eyes. "There's no one else to ask, Mr. Mackenzie. I wouldn't expect you to raise her, but you've done adoption cases, worked with a lot of kids. You'd find her a good home."

"Her?" he'd asked.

"Her. I had a sonogram. It's a girl." Marion had

smiled then and run her hand lightly across her stomach, a small caress filled with love.

That's when he realized he couldn't say no.

The memory still hit Mac hard. At that moment he'd envied the unborn baby. Her mother had wanted her so much. Marion O'Keefe had loved her child before she was even born. She'd worried about the baby's future and had trusted him to see to that future if she couldn't.

In the end, he didn't have the heart to refuse her request. He'd agreed to act as her unborn child's guardian if anything should happen to her, and then dismissed the entire incident. After all, Marion O'Keefe had been young and seemed healthy. No one could have predicted the aneurism that had taken her life.

Mac felt a stab of sorrow for the woman's passing, for the baby who would never know how loved she'd been before she was even born.

He might not have thought it would come to this, but the baby was his responsibility. He wasn't going to fail Marion or her child. Marion's baby would never know her mother's love, but Mac would see to it she was placed in a home where she would know love. He wouldn't trust her care to strangers. Until he found her a new home, he'd watch over the baby.

"I promised her mother and I have an ethical obligation to personally see to the baby."

"But—"

"Ms. Lindsay, unless you can come up with a legal reason why I can't take the child, then this conversation is over."

The woman sighed. "Would you at least take my card and phone if you need anything?"

"Listen, I might be stubborn," he flashed her a smile, hoping to charm her out of her annoyance, "but I'm not stupid."

He took the card. "I'll call regardless and let you know how we're doing and what I decide."

"Fine. There wasn't much at the apartment. Not even a crib for the baby. I don't think her mother had much."

"I don't either," Mac said. "I offered to write her will pro bono, but she refused."

Marion O'Keefe had been a proud, loving woman. She'd made payments. Five dollars every week, like clockwork.

Mac would make sure Katie knew that about her mother.

"The super said he'd pack all her personal items and ship them to you for Katie."

"That's fine."

The social worker started toward the door. "Mr. Mackenzie, do you know what you're getting yourself into?"

"She's how old?" he asked, knowing it was less than a year since Marion O'Keefe had sat in his office.

Ms. Lindsay glanced at her chart again. "Seven months."

"Seven months." He laughed. "How hard could it be?"

This time it was Kim Lindsay who laughed. "I'll talk to you in a couple days and you can let me know your answer then."

Ms. Thomas came back down the hall, carrying a bag. "I put her clothes and stuff in here. There's only two more diapers, so you'd better stop and get some."

"Thank you, Ms. Thomas." He took the bag.

"Let me go get her."

It would have been so much easier if Mac had allowed Ms. Lindsay to place the baby with someone who had experience with children. Social Services shouldn't have much trouble finding someone to adopt a baby.

Yet, he couldn't entrust her care to someone else.

He might not know this baby, but he knew that she was special.

So, he'd find a loving home for her. Someplace where she'd never want for anything, emotionally or financially.

"Here she is," said Ms. Thomas. She held the baby in a clean, soft blanket that looked out of place in the run-down apartment.

Mac took it and looked down at an angelic-looking face. Sleeping, her thumb tucked into the corner of her mouth, Katie O'Keefe was a beautiful baby. He ran a finger across her small pudgy cheek and something inside him twisted. She was so small, so vulnerable.

He pulled the blanket away from her head and revealed an amazing shock of red hair. She reminded him of her mother. He felt a surge of sympathy for this baby who would never know her mother, would never remember how much she was loved.

He'd find her a home—the perfect home. Until he did, he'd watch out for her.

"Thank you again, Ms. Thomas."

The old woman humphed an inarticulate reply.

Mac started toward the door.

What on earth was he going to do now? He'd assured the social worker and the baby-sitter that he could handle this. He knew the child had immediate needs, but he didn't even know where to begin.

He needed help.

But asking for help wasn't Mac's forte.

He tried to imagine who he could go to. He could call Mrs. Z., who was the closest thing he had to a mother, but she was in Pittsburgh. Not that he doubted she'd come help, but he couldn't impose on her.

The head of the firm, Leland Wagner, had grown daughters, or maybe even his wife would give him some pointers. But the idea of going to Mrs. Wagner for help didn't sit well.

There were other women attorneys and wives of attorneys at the firm. He could call one of them and ask for help in getting the baby settled.

He tried to concentrate on asking one of them, but the whole time, a mental image kept forming in his mind. It wasn't an attorney, or a spouse.

It was Amelia Gallagher.

Why on earth had asking her for help even crossed his mind? She didn't like him and went out of her way to show it. Which was fine, because he didn't like her either.

Oh, she was a beautiful woman…very beautiful. But she didn't seem to notice it. She was completely unaffected. But any red-blooded man noticed. Short blond hair and amazing blue eyes. Pleasant enough features. But that was just a laundry list of Amelia's physical attributes.

They weren't why she was beautiful.

It was her smile. He swore when her lips moved to the small upturned curve, it shot something right into her eyes and actually made them shine.

Katie made a small noise, interrupting Mac's thoughts, which was a good thing, because to the best of his knowledge he'd never thought anyone had shining eyes before. And he sincerely hoped he never did again.

Shining had nothing to do with his point.

Katie gurgled.

"What is my point?" he asked her.

She gurgled again.

His point was, Amelia was a woman, so she must know something about babies. And he'd pay her. Goodness knows she always snapped at the chance to work overtime.

Paying her.

Hiring someone to help was better than asking someone for a favor.

Mac realized he'd reached his car. He looked down at the baby, the bag and car seat.

How on earth was he going to manage all of this?

It was four fifty-five. Five more minutes and Mia could call it quits.

Thank goodness.

This had been a long, exhausting day.

First the copier had broken down.

Then the copier repair guy said he couldn't possibly come repair it until Monday, which meant half the firm came down to her desk clamoring for copies of life-or-death documents. So, Mia had forgone her lunch hour and taken a stack of papers to a neighboring copy center.

Phone calls, messages, and then there was the one distraught woman who'd left the office in tears. She hadn't said what the problem was, but it had taken Mia a good fifteen minutes to get her calmed down.

The only highlight of her day was her argument with Mac.

Four minutes.

Mia stood and started to straighten up her desk.

A hot bath.

With bubbles and a good book.

Oh, she had such plans for the evening.

She pulled her boots from the coat closet and slipped off her heels. They weren't the most elegant-looking boots, but Mia didn't care about elegance. She cared about warmth. The heater in her car was broken, and most days she was lucky if it warmed up enough to keep ice from forming on the front windshield. It never truly got warm enough to take the chill off.

She slipped on her boots.

Three minutes to go.

"Night, Amelia," Donovan and a couple other attorneys called as they all headed out together.

"Night."

Two minutes.

Leland Wagner, the firm's senior partner followed close on their heels. "You'll lock up, dear?"

"Sure thing."

"Would you like me to stay and make sure your car starts?"

Her battery had died last week and she'd had to wait for AAA to come and jump start her car. "No, sir. I had a new battery put in. I should be fine."

"Very well. Good night, and drive carefully."

"You, too."

Five o'clock.

She was out of here.

She bundled into a sweater, and then her thin jacket.

Maybe before she bought a new car she'd buy a new coat.

Ah, but if she had a new car, she wouldn't need a new coat. If she got the auto-ignition and seat-warmers it would be toasty before she ever got out there.

Pondering which was the wiser course, she wrapped her scarf around her neck again and again, then stuffed a woolen hat on her head.

Feeling stiff beneath her layers, she picked up her bag and walked toward the front door. She flipped on the security alarm, and then let herself out, checking that everything was locked up tight.

The world was white.

Snow was falling in big, thick flakes. There was at least a couple inches of snow since she'd left the office at lunch. It wasn't a blizzard yet, but she had no problem imagining it turning into one.

Mia had just started down the steps when a blue Explorer pulled up at the curb.

The passenger window descended. "Amelia, I'm glad you're still here," Mac called.

"What did you need, Larry," she said.

"I need you," he replied, not even commenting on her use of his first name.

Mia managed to keep from choking at his reply, but barely. "Pardon me?"

"Not *you,* your help," he corrected himself. "Get in the car, please?"

"But—"

"*Please,* Amelia?"

There was something in his voice that told Mia that now was not the time to argue or taunt him. Something was wrong.

She waddled her well-layered self toward the car, and as she got closer she heard noise. Lots of noise. It wasn't music. Or if it was, it was the most awful music ever.

It sounded like—

She opened the door and peeked in the back seat.

It was.

A baby.

And a crying baby, at that.

Chapter Two

"What did you do now, Larry?" Mia accused loudly as she leaned into the car and stared at the car seat.

"Just get in and buckle up, fast. She cries whenever the car stops. If it's moving, she's okay."

Mac had learned that the hard way. The entire trip from Esther Thomas's home to the office was fraught with red lights.

As a matter of fact, every single traffic light he came to was red. And it stayed red for an inordinately long period of time.

Or maybe it just seemed like eternity because Katie O'Keefe screamed every time the car stopped.

Speaking of eternity, he watched Mia settle herself in the passenger seat, taking more time than he liked. She was moving rather stiffly.

"Are you in yet?" he asked, practically shouting to be heard over the baby.

She nodded.

Mac threw the car in gear and started down the street. The baby quieted immediately.

"So, what's going on, Mac?" Mia asked, obviously disconcerted enough not to tease him.

As a matter of fact, she sounded genuinely concerned.

"You know that call you took today? That woman, Kim Lindsay? She was calling to tell me I had a baby."

"Oh, Larry, how could you be so careless?"

He glared at her. "I wasn't, but of course you'd assume the worst. Kim Lindsay is the social worker. I'm the baby's guardian."

She was silent a moment, then softly said, "I'm sorry for jumping to conclusions."

Amelia Gallagher apologizing? That was certainly out of character.

He nodded his acceptance and concentrated on the driving. He didn't even glance in her direction as he said, "A woman came into the office last year wanting me to draw up a will. She named me her executor and guardian of her unborn child. I know it's not normally the way things are handled, asking a lawyer to serve as guardian. It's not something I'd normally agree to, but…" he paused. "There was something about her, about her story. She had no family, the baby's father had died, and top it off, she was new in town. She was completely alone in the world. She worked at the courthouse and had heard about some of the cases I've done involving kids and…well, I just couldn't say no."

Mac had felt the now familiar stab of empathy for Marion O'Keefe.

He remembered her vividly, even after all this time. She'd been pale. More pale than redheads normally were. He should have known something was wrong with her physically. He should have tried to help her.

Kim Lindsay said that she'd died of a brain aneurism. It was fast and painless. There was nothing anyone could have done. But Mac still felt guilty, as if he should have known and been able to do something.

His voice lowered. "I never really expected it to come to anything. She passed away yesterday and this is her daughter."

"Oh, the poor baby." Mia peeked into the back seat.

Mac was pretty sure he caught the glitter of a tear in her eye, but she brushed her hand across her face, so he wasn't sure.

"What can I do?" she asked.

He'd expected he'd have to cajole her, to bribe her…heck, maybe even threaten her into helping. He hadn't expected such an immediate offer of assistance.

"I don't know anything about babies," he admitted.

"I don't know much myself. I mean, I've baby-sat, so, I guess I know more than you, but it's been years. I'm no expert."

"Do you know enough to help me buy what she needs? At least, enough to cover her most immediate needs? She's only got two diapers and one bottle of formula. There wasn't much in the apartment, not even a crib. I know what they sent with me won't get me through the night, much less the next couple days. I can pay you."

Amelia glared at him, as if she was insulted. He knew it wouldn't take him long to annoy her. Even when he wasn't trying, annoying Amelia came pretty easily to him.

"I don't need your money," she said, frowning at him.

The baby made a soft cooing noise in the back and Amelia's expression softened. "But I suppose I can help you get set up. Does this mean you're keeping her?"

The light ahead of them turned red, and as the car stopped, right on schedule, Katie started to scream.

When they started moving again and the baby quieted, he answered, "No, of course not. I mean, I'm not equipped to take care of a baby for a few days, much less, take care of her long-term."

"So why didn't you just let that Kim Lindsay take her? That's what Social Services does, right?"

His stomach clenched at the thought of sending Katie O'Keefe into the foster system, even if it would be only for a short time. He remembered what it was like being shuttled from house to house. Not that he was in the foster care system, unless you referred to his extended family in that respect.

When he was ten his parents took off for California with dreams of fame and glory, at least that's what they said. Mac had always felt as if they'd simply become bored with playing a family. They'd sent him to live at his grandmother's for a short stay. They'd promised to send for him, but they never did. Oh, he got an occasional call or letter, always filled with empty promises. His parents couldn't handle the responsibility of a kid.

His grandmother passed away when he was twelve, he stayed with his aunt for a year, but she wasn't thrilled with having the responsibility of looking after a child.

Finally, he ended up moving in with a friend's family during his freshman year of school. The Zumigalas had let him stay until he left for college. Despite the fact they'd treated him as a son, he'd always known he wasn't. He'd always known he was living there at their discretion and any day they could decide to kick him out. He'd expected it, had waited for it. But they never had.

They still invited him *home* to Pittsburgh for every holiday. They were the closest thing Mac had to a family.

He had never understood why they'd taken a stranger into their home, taken on the responsibility of another child. After all, his own family didn't want him, why had they?

He'd never really figured it out. But he was thankful. They had given him more than a house to live in, they'd given him a home.

He was going to find for Katie O'Keefe what the Zumigalas had given him...stability. A place to belong.

She might be too young to understand on an intellectual level how precarious her position was, but she'd have to recognize what was happening on an emotional level. And he wouldn't do that to her.

No, she'd stay with him until he found her a family of her own. A permanent family. People who would love her and never desert her.

"Her mother left her to my care," he said. "She trusted me to find her a suitable family, though neither of us really expected me to ever be in charge of the baby. But I am, and I will personally care for her until other arrangements can be made."

"What kind of arrangements?" Amelia asked softly.

"I'll find some family to adopt her. I mean, how hard can it be? She's a beautiful baby. She's only seven-months-old. There has to be hundreds of prospective families who would love to make her their daughter."

Another red light, and the car filled with the baby's screams.

"Do you think she's hungry?"

"I don't know. Basically, the old lady watching her just handed her and that diaper bag to me."

"Why don't you pull over somewhere and let's try feeding her. Maybe she'd be happier then?"

"Okay." He'd do anything to calm the baby down. Her pitiful wails were breaking his heart.

He pulled into a gas station. "I need to fill the tank anyway. I think the weather reports were right, and I want the tank topped off if it's going to storm."

Mac got out and started pumping the gas. He watched Amelia get out and climb into the back seat with the baby. He couldn't help glancing in the back window as she opened up the diaper bag and found the bottle. She leaned over and started feeding Katie.

He watched her lean closer to the baby, saying something, though he couldn't make out just what. She was smiling at the baby. He knew, even though she was looking at Katie and not at him, that her eyes were sparkling. Alight with that special something she had—that certain quality Amelia Gallagher had, that drew people to her.

Even babies.

Donovan once said she was gregarious and friendly, the perfect receptionist. Maybe. Though describing Amelia as gregarious might be accurate to his colleague, she'd never been overly friendly with Mac.

As a matter of fact, she'd been almost hostile.

She always picked at him.

Of course, he picked right back. Their banterish quarrels were well-known in the office.

Why did she always rub him the wrong way?

Mac realized the gas had stopped pumping. He replaced the nozzle, put the cap back on the tank and walked into the store to pay, still puzzling over Amelia and how she affected him.

Mia watched Mac disappear into the store. He'd been staring at her.

"What's up with him, Katie?" she whispered.

There had been something in his voice as he spoke about Katie. Something that told her there was more to this situation than his wanting to find the baby a home. There had been an undercurrent of pain, of vulnerability, in his tone. She'd never heard anything like that before.

She knew that Larry did a lot of volunteer work. She'd always thought it was just a way for him to fulfill the firm's requirement that each lawyer give back to the community by doing pro bono work. But now she wondered if there was something more to it.

Katie slurped enthusiastically at her bottle.

She'd been hungry. Very hungry if her speed at emptying it was any indication.

"Didn't they feed you?" she asked.

Katie smiled without letting go of the bottle's nipple. Milk bubbles formed at the gap.

"You are sweet," Mia told her.

Katie gurgled her agreement just as Mac opened the door and got in. "Are you ready?"

"Sure. I'll sit back here and let Katie finish her bottle before we get to the store."

"Fine."

It was almost a relief to be in the back with Katie. This way she didn't have to deal with Mac looking at her.

It wasn't as if she was shy, but he always made her feel as if he saw…

Well, she wasn't sure what he saw, but whatever it was, it made her uncomfortable.

Almost as uncomfortable as her new questions about Mac's motivations.

She looked at the baby and couldn't help remember when her brothers were little. Her mother had let her feed them, just like she was feeding Katie now.

"You're responsible for him, Mia," her mother had told her. She'd been hardly more than a baby herself, but she'd taken care of first Marty, then Ryan.

After her father finally left, she tried to help her mother take care of the boys. Even though she was only a few years older than they were, she assumed more of a parental role than a sister's.

But now that Ryan had graduated her job was done. She could do all the things she'd dreamed about. It wasn't just a new car. She could travel.

Maybe even date.

Nothing serious. Mia didn't want anything serious or committed. She wanted fun. She wanted adventure. She wanted to live out her dreams…if she could ever figure out what they were.

She sighed.

"You're awfully quiet back there?"

She forced herself to put away thoughts of the past. It was better to concentrate on here and now.

"After all Katie's screaming are you really complaining that it's too quiet?"

"No," he said with a laugh. "Listen, after we shop, would you come back to my house and help, just for a while? I have to get a crib and whatever else she'll need for however long I have her. Everything will need to be set up and I'll need help with her. I mean, I'll take you back to the office once it's all settled so you can get your car."

"Sure," Mia said, without thinking. "In for a penny, in for a pound."

A couple hours later, the car was stuffed with multiple pounds of baby paraphernalia. Mac had bought out the baby store. Watching him mull over the merits of different baby monitors, trying to decide what size Onesies to buy…well, it had been cute.

And thinking the word cute as a description for Larry Mackenzie was just too strange for Mia. She just wanted to go home and forget this odd afternoon.

She was back in the front seat as they pulled into Mac's driveway. Almost done, she thought with a sigh as he put the car in Park and turned off the ignition.

She studied his house. It wasn't at all what she'd expected, though she couldn't really have said what it was she did expect.

It was a neat, two-story brick home in Glenwood Hills, a lovely, older section of town. A huge tree stood dead-center in the front yard. In the summer it probably shaded the whole house. Right now, it stood like a snowy sentinel.

"Come on," he said. "If you get Katie out, I'll start unpacking the stuff."

Doing so would probably take him a while. For a man who claimed he was giving the baby up, he'd bought more than what the baby would need for the next year.

A crib, a changing table, clothes, bottles, pacifiers, toys, stuffed animals, diapers—three different sizes because they weren't sure what size she'd need—and formula.

"Come on, Katie," Mia said as she unstrapped the seat.

"Here," Mac said, tossing her the keys.

Mia carried the baby onto the porch, set the car seat down on the ground and unlocked the door.

"Switches are to your left," Mac hollered.

Mia flipped the two switches there. One turned on the porch light, and one turned on a table lamp next to a dark leather couch. She kicked off her shoes and walked to the couch and set the car seat on it.

She studied the living room. The focal points were a huge fireplace and a piano. Did that mean Mac played the piano, or was it just for show?

He had a huge leather couch and a matching overstuffed chair with a knobby-looking afghan thrown carelessly over the back. And there was a picture on the wall. No, not a picture, a painting. It was an outdoor scene. A rustic-looking barn in a snowy setting.

There was a thump on the door, and Mia remembered Mac was bringing in boxes. She ran and opened the door for him.

"Sorry."

"No problem. I'm going to just haul everything to

the guest room. Katie can use that for a room while she's here."

"Do you need help?"

"Let me get the little stuff first, then you can help me get the crib."

"Okay." She watched him make his way up the staircase to the left of the door and then turned her attention back to Katie. "Hey, you. Let's get you unbundled."

She unzipped the little sack that fit over the seat and acted as a coat.

"There you are," she cooed as the baby burbled more happy little bubbles at her. "Oh, you're going to melt some hearts, let me tell you."

"Does she answer back?" Mac asked with a hint of laughter in his voice.

"No. Babies don't generally talk at this age."

"I thought you weren't an expert."

"I'm not, but you said she was seven months. I don't think they really talk until they're older than that."

"Oh."

"I'm going to leave her in the car seat until I'm done helping you. I don't want her to get into trouble, and I might know she doesn't talk, but I'm not sure if babies crawl at this age."

She hurried to the door. The faster she helped Mac get the baby settled, the faster she could get out of here. This personal glimpse at Mac's home was leaving her feeling…unsettled. She didn't know why.

Somehow it was easier to picture him living in a sterile, bachelor pad, than this cozy little place. It felt warm, yet lived-in here. It felt…almost comfortable.

Homey.

Homey and Larry Mackenzie?

Now those were two thoughts she never imagined going together.

They carried the box for the crib into the guest room. Again, the room didn't fit Mia's mental picture of what Mac should have. It had a quilt on a double bed, and old family photos decorating the walls.

There was even a sampler.

Mia would have liked a chance to study all these bits and pieces of Mac, but she couldn't figure out why she'd want to. His house might not be what she'd imagined it to be, but that didn't mean Mac wasn't the most annoying human she'd ever met.

"I'll just leave you to it," she said and hurried back to the baby. She freed Katie from the car seat while Mac went to work on the crib.

"I love your hair, sweetie," she cooed, toying with a tiny little ringlet. "Men have a thing for redheads."

"They like blondes too," Mac said.

Mia looked up and saw Mac standing at the bottom of the stairway.

The man moved like a cat.

"What are you doing now?" she asked, ignoring his comment on blondes.

"Going for some tools. But I hate to have you lie to the baby. Some men do have a thing for redheads, but some of us prefer blondes."

"I…" Mia didn't know what to say to a statement like that.

If it was any other man in the world, she'd think he was flirting with her. But Mac didn't like her any more than she liked him, so she was sure it wasn't flirting.

"Stop lurking and finish up. It's going on eight. I need to get home and you need to get this baby into bed."

Mac glanced at his watch, as if he didn't believe she could tell time. "I can't believe it's this late already."

He walked through the room and into the kitchen. She could hear a door open and then the sound of his footsteps on stairs.

"What do you think of him?" she asked the baby.

Katie gurgled a response and stiffened.

"Oh, you want to stand up, do you?" Mia held the baby under her arms and Katie pushed herself up. "It won't be long until you're toddling all over the place. I wonder if you're crawling yet?"

She looked at the pile of shopping bags Mac had brought in.

"I know we bought a couple blankets," she told Katie. Still holding the baby, she dug through the bags and found one. "Here you go."

She laid it on the floor and placed Katie on it.

Then put a few of her new toys down as well, just a little out of reach. The baby crept right up to them.

"Well, look at that. You do crawl," Mia said with a laugh, just as Mac came back into the room.

"She crawls," she told him.

"Yeah?" He knelt down beside Mia, close, but not quite touching her.

"Watch." She moved a few of the toys farther away and Katie immediately inched her way toward them.

They both admired her progress. His hand draped carelessly over Mia's shoulder, as if he was using her to prop himself up. She snuck a peek. His eyes were glued to the baby's movements, a slight smile played on his lips.

The moment felt special…almost intimate.

The thought shook Mia. So she leaned over and picked up Katie and wrinkled her nose.

"Have you ever changed a diaper before?" she asked Mac.

He clutched the toolbox as if it were a shield. "No, but that's okay, you go ahead. I'll just go set up her crib so we can take you to your car."

"Oh, no. I'm supposed to help you get settled. What are you going to do when I'm not here? I don't have to be an expert to know that babies need changing…a lot."

Mac looked as if she'd told him he was about to face a firing squad. Mia couldn't contain a small chuckle. "Come on, you need to learn."

"I'll just watch this time. Then I can figure it out later."

"No, I'll watch while you figure it out."

"I uh…"

"Put down the toolbox and come here."

Mac complied, but with obvious reluctance. Slowly, he sat on the floor next to her and stared at the baby as if she were some wild, dangerous animal.

Mia dug out a diaper and a box of wipes they'd just bought. "Here, start with these."

Mac straightened his shoulders and looked determined. "I deal with complex legal issues and distraught clients all day. I can learn to do this."

Mia held back her smile as he diapered the baby with all the seriousness of a lawyer giving a closing argument.

"Now, just use those little tapes to hold it in place," she said as he finished.

"It's not tape, it's Velcro," he said as he finished with flourish. "There. One happily diapered baby."

"Velcro?" Mia said. "Back in my day, it was tape. Now, I'm feeling old."

He gave a little scoff. "You're not old."

"I didn't say I was, Larry. I just said I *felt* old. Now, you, you're old."

He shot her a look. "You make me sound ancient."

"Aren't you?" she asked, grinning.

"Thirty isn't exactly ancient."

"Thirty. My, my, my." She clutched a hand to her chest. "You're almost beyond ancient."

"And just how old are you?" he asked.

"Twenty-seven."

Twenty-seven and finally ready to start living. She was going to fulfill all her dreams—as soon as she settled on just what they were. No matter what, she was free to pursue them all. She clung to the thought a moment and savored it.

"I can see how those three years make a difference."

"A big, huge, difference." She laughed.

He looked at the baby and said, "She's crazy, you know that already, don't you? Sure you do. I can tell what a bright girl you are, Katie-did."

Katie gurgled her response.

"I think she said girls stick together, and you're the crazy one," Mia said. "But even though we doubt your sanity, you are officially capable of diapering an infant."

"Thanks for the help," he said. "After that diaper, I think I can handle anything."

The baby gave a small whimper and Mia held out her hands. Mac handed Katie over without protest.

"Could you see if you could find her pacifier?" Mia asked, as she patted the baby's back.

He unclipped it from the car seat and handed it to Mia. His hand brushed hers. It was just a small touch,

so quick that if it had been someone else she probably wouldn't have even noticed it.

But it wasn't someone else, it was Mac. She noticed just about everything about him.

Most of it was annoying, she reminded herself.

But his touch…well, it wasn't.

She gave herself a mental shake and clipped the
pacifier to the baby's sleeper. "You know, I'm sure
it wasn't a mother or father who came up with the
idea for a pacifier clip, it was an older sister who got
tired of hunting for them."

"How much older are you than your brothers?"

"I'm three years older than Marty and five years
older than Ryan. Ryan just graduated from college
with his B.A. in education."

"Good for him."

"Yeah." Suddenly it struck her that the conversation was moving dangerously close to personal and
she quickly pulled back. "Mac, why don't you go get
that crib together. I really do have to get home soon."

She was starving. She'd worked her way through
lunch and it was way past supper time.

"Okay."

He hurried out of the room and Mia felt relieved.
First that weird reaction to his touch, then an almost
personal conversation. They'd exchanged ages, and
she'd talked of her brothers.

Chatting with Mac. It was just too odd.

She blamed it on low blood-sugar.

It was time to get home.

Amelia had called him Mac. He was pretty sure she hadn't meant to, or even realized she'd done it, but she had.

He dropped in the bolt that held the crib's side in place, wondering at the small glimpses he'd had of Amelia-the-person, not just Amelia-the-thorn- in-his-side.

He'd watched her cooing over the baby. Even now, a floor away, he could hear her.

She was singing something.

If you'd asked him yesterday, he wouldn't have believed that not only would Amelia agree to help him, but that she'd be sitting in his living room sing-ing to a baby.

He got up and dropped the mattress into the fin-ished crib, then hurried downstairs to Amelia.

"The crib's together and I think I can handle the rest, so anytime you're ready."

"Let me just finish giving Katie this bottle, then I'll let you take me back."

He sat down across from her. "Amelia?"

"Mia," she corrected.

"Mia?"

"Yes. I've been Amelia for way too many years. I'm going back to Mia."

"Mia." He studied her a moment. "It suits you."

He could have ignored her wish, gotten even with her for all the times she'd called him Larry, but looking at her, he saw that for some reason this name change meant something…something important. Even if he didn't owe her—which he did—he wouldn't squash whatever it was it meant.

"Mia," he said again, "I just want to thank you for all the help. I mean—"

"Don't worry about it. I figure that this means you owe me one, and I'll be sure to find some way to make you pay."

He chuckled. "I'm sure you will."

She turned her attention to the baby, and Mac leaned back and simply watched her. It was a pleasant occupation.

If he'd met her at a party, he'd get her number as quickly as possible. He'd call, they'd date and he'd break it off before it got too serious.

Just like he was sure he didn't want kids, Mac was sure he didn't want a messy long-term relationship. He'd decided long ago he was better off relying on himself.

Despite his good intentions, he could want Mia Gallagher—at least for a while—if she was someone else. But he worked with her, and for some reason, she didn't like him. Two good reasons not to allow this physical attraction to go anywhere.

But if things were different, then maybe.

"Mac, I said, I think she's done." Mia had the baby propped against her shoulder and was patting her back. "Anytime you're ready, I'm set."

"Oh, yeah, sure."

Mia got up and put the baby in her car seat before rebundling herself in her layers.

"Why don't you just wear a warmer coat and skip the walking closet look?" he asked.

"Do you really think the way I dress is any of your concern, Larry?"

He was back to being Larry which meant he'd annoyed her. "I didn't mean that the way it came out. It's just even with layers you don't look warm enough."

"Well, for your information, I was just thinking about buying a new coat today."

"But winter's almost over."

"You could have fooled me."

He opened the door and was greeted by a wall of white. He couldn't even see the end of the porch. There was no way he was taking a baby out in this. Even without a baby, he'd be a fool to try to drive in this kind of storm.

"It looks like you're the winner. Winter's not quite ready to give up without a fight. It also looks as if you're spending the night."

Chapter Three

"It looks like you're spending the night. That storm has hit with a vengeance."

Mia heard Mac say the words, but refused to believe them.

"It can't be that bad," she said as she walked to the front door and peeked out.

Her heart sank as she looked out at the gusts of snow. She couldn't even see the house across the street.

"Oh," she said.

"Yeah, oh." Mac sounded as glum as she felt.

"But I can't stay here."

She wanted to be home in her safe little apartment.

She wanted to curl up with a good book under a quilt.

She did not want to deal with Larry Mackenzie who didn't look anymore enthusiastic about the plan than she did.

"If it were just the two of us, I just might risk trying to get you home," he said. "But do you really want to take Katie out in this?"

"No," she said as she reached out and shut the door, realizing she was defeated.

Utterly, horribly foiled.

More than anything she wanted to go home, to forget the new insights she'd had into who Larry Mackenzie really was. Things she'd prefer not knowing. Things that made her feel decidedly uncomfortable.

Squabbling with Mac, feeling annoyed by him, was so much easier than feeling…she wasn't sure what this was, but it was definitely a softer feeling. Warm and…

No way was she feeling warmly toward Mac. Not even lukewarmly. She glanced at him and a heat coursed through her veins.

She shut off the thought and tried to will herself to be as cold as the storm outside.

Mac was talking. "…I set Katie's crib up in the guest room, but the bed's still there. I'll sleep there and be close to her, you can take my bed."

Sleep in Mac's bed? Be wrapped in the same

sheets that touched his body every night? She felt a warm flush flood her body.

It was too intimate.

She couldn't do it.

She wouldn't do it.

No way.

Visions of the current snowstorm couldn't cool down the way that made her feel.

"No. Thanks anyway," she added. "I'll sleep with Katie."

Mac looked stubborn. "You'd be much more comfortable—"

"Sleeping with Katie," she finished for him. "That's final."

He looked like he might argue more, then thought better of it.

"Fine," he said with a shrug. "Whatever. How about I make some dinner for us? I don't know about you, but I'm starving."

"I am hungry," she admitted cautiously. "Maybe you'd rather I made dinner?"

"You doubt my cooking abilities?" he asked with a note of challenge in his voice.

"Not doubt so much as I'm just too hungry to take a risk."

"Chicken," he said, teasingly.

"Yeah, maybe."

"You go get Katie out of her seat and I'll take care of dinner. Trust me."

"Sure, I'll trust you…about as far as I can throw you."

Amelia—no, take that back, Mia—was grumbling something soft and low to the baby as Mac went into the kitchen. He knew he didn't want to know what she was saying.

It probably had something to do with him…and it definitely wasn't complimentary.

He chuckled. Sparring with Mia kept him sharp.

Mia.

He smiled as he thought of her new name. He wasn't sure what the significance was, but he was sure that Mia suited her.

Now to find something to make for dinner that would do more than suit her. He wanted to wow her.

Unfortunately, wowing wasn't generally in the kitchen when he was.

Edible maybe—if he was lucky—but wowing?

He opened the cupboard and stared at its contents, willing some great meal idea to come to him. Nothing wow-able in there. He opened the refrigerator.

Eggs.

He had a whole dozen eggs.

And on the second shelf, towards the back, was a

container of cheese. He lifted the lid. Nothing was growing on it, so it must be good.

An omelette.

He could make an omelette, and of all the things he could cook, it probably had the most wow-able potential.

An omelette, even a good one, wasn't exactly wow-able on its own. He needed something to go with it.

He remembered the Italian bread. He buttered it, applied a bit of garlic salt, and topped it with some of the cheese, then popped it in the oven before he started on the eggs.

Whisking eggs gave him time to think. The realization that he had not just a woman, but a baby in his living room, hit him.

Today had been a whirlwind of change. When he left the house this morning he hadn't known what he was in for. He beat the eggs with a little more force than necessary.

First thing Monday morning he'd have to start the process of finding Katie O'Keefe a home. Finding her parents. A family. People who would love her no matter what.

People who would never leave.

It would have to be an open adoption. He'd only use an agency that would let him participate in the process. He wouldn't entrust her care to just anyone.

He wanted to make sure her financial needs were always met. Marion hadn't been able to provide much in the way of a cushion for the baby. Maybe there was life insurance?

He'd check and sort through Marion's estate.

But no matter what, Katie would be cared for. He'd start a trust for her himself. He had plenty of money and no one to spend it on.

He poured the egg mixture on the skillet.

Yeah, he liked the idea.

Katie wouldn't have to work and scrounge her way through school like he did. She'd have a college fund waiting for her.

When Marion O'Keefe asked him to act as guardian for her unborn baby, he'd surprised himself by saying yes. He'd only met the woman twice. First when she'd come in to talk about the will, and a second time when she came in and signed everything. Twice. That's all. But he felt connected to her.

He'd asked himself why, why he'd said yes to acting as guardian, and why he'd felt a bond with Marion O'Keefe. The only answer he'd been able to come up with was that in Marion he'd seen himself. Someone on their own.

Someone alone.

And now he was in charge of her daughter.

He'd do his best to see that Katie O'Keefe was never alone. He'd see to it, just like he'd see to it she had the best parents in the world. People who would love her no matter what. People who'd have time for her, who would revel in her every success.

He'd do it for Marion O'Keefe.

He'd do it for Katie.

And maybe, if he was honest, he'd do it for himself.

When he was lost and on his own the Zumigalas had taken him in. It felt as if he was paying back some of that debt by helping Katie.

"Hey, Larry," Amelia said as she came into the kitchen, pulling him abruptly from his thoughts. "That doesn't smell half bad."

"I hope cheese omelettes are okay? I was starving and wanted something fast."

"Sounds perfect," she said agreeably.

Too agreeably.

Mia Gallagher was not an agreeable person.

The only thing that saved him from being nervous about her niceness was that she'd called him Larry.

"There's a bottle of wine in the fridge if you'd like a glass," he said.

"Sure. Glasses?"

"Over the sink," he said. He tried not to notice that when she stood on tip-toe and reached for the glasses her shirt hiked up revealing a small swatch of white stomach.

After all, it was less than an inch of skin. He saw more skin than that just about anywhere these days.

But that small flash made him feel something that, if it had been any other woman, he'd have to say was desire.

But desiring Mia was out of the question.

It was absurd.

Most days they were adversaries. They'd simply called a truce today for Katie's sake. When the storm was over, he was sure things would go back to normal. So no staring at that small patch of skin and wondering if it was as soft as it looked.

He forced himself to concentrate on the omelette.

"Here we go," she said, setting the glasses down and pouring the wine.

She handed him one and their fingers grazed, just the barest contact. But there it was, that feeling again. Since it couldn't be lust, the burning sensation had to be an ulcer.

Yeah, that was it.

Amelia Gallagher had finally given him an ulcer.

She'd probably given him high blood pressure as well, which would explain the weird, light-headed sensation he was having.

"I put Katie down in her crib," she said. "That was one tired baby."

The light-headedness was replaced by a spurt of panic.

The upstairs bedroom seemed miles away. What if the baby cried? What if she rolled over and suffocated?

What if she got stuck in the bars of the crib.

What if—

As if sensing his apprehension, she added, "She's sound asleep. She's fine."

"Did you turn on the monitor?" he asked, wondering if he should go up and check on the baby.

She laughed. "Yes. I set the receiver on the table."

Mac gave a sigh of relief. He hadn't noticed the receiver when she came in. Probably because when Mia entered a room he didn't notice anything but her.

Not in a woman-sort of way, but rather in an annoying-sort of way. She was like an itch he could never quite scratch. It was just there, driving him quietly mad.

Yeah. Driving him mad. That was Mia.

"Is it turned up loud enough that we can hear her?"

"It's on high." She picked it up and held to her ear. "You can hear her breathing if you listen carefully."

"Good." The baby was breathing. That was one less thing to worry about.

He concentrated on the omelette, which was easier than concentrating on Mia.

They'd apparently used up all their conversation. Mac didn't know what else to say to fill the quiet. Which was fine with him.

Mia sat down at the kitchen table and watched him flip the omelette.

He glanced at her. She was sipping the wine, looking totally at home. A slight smile played on her face. He wondered what she was thinking, not that he'd ask.

"You know what I was thinking?" she asked. Once again, almost as if she'd read his mind.

"Hmm?" he said, trying not to sound overly interested, because he wasn't interested in what Mia was thinking.

"I was remembering when I was a kid. There was a storm like this one Christmas Eve. It was horrible. Everything shut down. Nothing was moving. That was the bad part." She left the story hanging a moment.

Mac asked, "But there was a good part?"

"Oh, yeah. A very good part. My mom was scheduled to work that night. They were paying time- and-a-half, and we really needed the extra money. But the storm shut everything down and she couldn't get in. We lost out on the overtime, but in the end we got something worth so much more. It was as if there was no one else in the world. We were together. That was everything. We had this marathon game of 500 rummy. I think we took it way over a thousand."

A small smile whispered across her lips. Her eyes got a faraway gaze.

Mac wouldn't have admitted it to anyone, but the sight was mesmerizing. He was enthralled, caught up in her remembrance.

"Ryan was still little, so he was my partner," she

continued. "We made hot chocolate. We all fell asleep in the living room. And Christmas morning the boys woke us up. Mom and I stayed under the covers and watched them open presents. There wasn't much—there never was. But they were so happy. We were all so happy. That's what this storm reminds me of. Home."

"Being stranded with me makes you think of home?" he asked, sure he'd heard wrong.

That startled her right out of her nostalgia. "Not you," she assured him. "The snow. I said the storm. That's what I meant. I like storms when I don't have to go out in them. They remind me of one of the best holidays I ever spent."

"Well, I'm glad it's not me." There was a feeling in the pit of Mac's stomach. It had to be relief. After all, he wouldn't want Mia feeling as if spending time with him reminded her of home. It would be nuts.

"I'd be certifiable if you gave me warm, fuzzy thoughts of home and being safe," she said, agreeing with him even if she didn't know she was agreeing with him.

"Well, you are certifiable," he said helpfully, giving her a little smile to let her know he was teasing.

She must have missed the teasing fact, though, because she simply glared at him and said, "Never mind. I'm sorry I said anything, *Larry*."

He should have told her that he was kidding, but to be honest, he preferred her annoyed.

He was actually thrilled she'd called him Larry. She'd said his name with that particular tone that she always used. The one guaranteed to set his teeth on edge, which was good, because for a moment, listening to her story, he'd almost felt warm and fuzzy.

That wasn't good.

Having her annoyed was better.

But as he pulled the cookie sheet of toast out of the oven and split the omelette and toast between two plates, he glanced at her rigid posture, her slight grimace and he felt…odd. He might not want to feel warm and fuzzy with Mia, but her annoyance didn't feel right either.

He set one of the plates in front of her, then sat down with his own.

"Thanks" was all Mia said.

Just one word, then silence.

Silence when Mia was in the room made him nervous. He was much more comfortable sniping with her and her sniping back. Mia wasn't the type to suffer silently.

He almost welcomed the small snuffle Katie made over the monitor.

"Do you think we should go check her?" he asked.

"She's fine."

Two words.

He was getting somewhere, although he still wasn't sure why he wanted to get anywhere at all.

"Tell me more about your family," he said.

"No, thank you."

Three words, but they didn't feel like progress. She was mad.

Mia spent a lot of time being mad when he was around, but for some reason this time it was different. He shouldn't have made that crack about her thinking of him as homey.

"Listen, I'm sorry."

She just shrugged.

"Okay, I have a storm story, too."

She didn't say anything, but did make eye contact. Mac took that as an invitation to continue.

"I grew up in a suburb of Pittsburgh, Bethel Park. We don't get nearly as much snow down there as Erie does. Moving two hours north doesn't seem like it should equate to such a huge difference snow-wise, but it does. I still don't think I've quite gotten used to the weather here."

She took another bite of her omelette. She didn't grimace while she chewed it, so she must like it, which was good. Too bad she didn't seem to be liking him.

"Anyway, we got clobbered by a storm my freshman year of high school. Everything was canceled. Now that I live in Erie, it seems odd—it takes a couple feet to shut things down here. But in Pittsburgh, those six inches of snow shut down the city. Chet and I decided to go sled-riding, only we didn't have any sleds."

"Chet?" she asked.

"A—" he hesitated "—friend."

Mac was never sure how to describe Chet and his parents. They were more than friends. More like family. But it was too hard to explain his relationship with them, so he settled for *friend.*

"We didn't have sleds. Too old and cool for them," he continued. "But we decided it was the perfect day for sledding."

"So what did you do?"

"We stole the old mattress his mom had in the garage and took it to the grade school around the corner. Pittsburgh might not get as much snow, but it has more than enough hills. This one was a whopper. Unfortunately, mattresses don't function real well as sleds. But Chet and I, we decided to get some garbage bags and duct tape. It took two rolls of duct tape, but we covered the mattress—slicked it up. We jumped on like it was a toboggan and took off down the hill."

He smiled at the memory.

"Sounds like fun," she said slowly.

She was talking to him again, and if he wasn't mistaken, there was a small smile playing on her lips. She must have forgiven him.

"It was fun," he agreed, encouraged. "We rode until the duct tape started to fall off. Then decided to try for one more ride. Well, we took it to the steepest part of the hill, jumped on…without really checking out the path we'd take."

"Uh, oh." She actually chuckled, knowing something must have happened.

"Yeah. *Uh, oh.* You see, there was this giant oak at the bottom of the hill. Wham."

"Were you both okay?"

"I broke my ankle, Chet broke his nose. He's still got a bump. Mrs. Z. tried to tell him it added character. I said it made him look like a prizefighter."

She laughed then.

The small sound filled the kitchen and some of the warmth she'd been talking about earlier spread through Mac. He should try to fight it, try to ignore it, but somehow he just couldn't work up the energy.

He laughed along with her.

And for the first time ever, they simply chatted, sharing bits and pieces of themselves with each other.

It left Mac feeling odd.

He couldn't quite identify the feeling, and finally gave up trying.

It was enough that they were getting along.

At least for now.

Chapter Four

Mia awoke with a start, sensing something was wrong. Someone was breathing, a soft little intake of air, followed by a small whoosh as they exhaled.

Someone who wasn't her was breathing.

And since no one else slept with her, that was wrong.

Slowly she opened her eyes and spotted the crib.

Katie.

A baby. A snowstorm. Omelettes. It all came rushing back.

She'd spent the night at Mac's.

She'd shared a dinner with him. They'd actually chatted and laughed as they did dishes together.

Then Katie had woken up and Mia had fed her and

put her back to bed, then gone to bed herself. In Mac's spare room. Wearing one of his old T-shirts.

She glanced at the clock.

It was seven.

Katie had slept through the night.

She should probably get up and grab a shower before the baby woke up. She lifted the edge of the cover, and immediately put it back down, conserving the warmth.

The heat must have gone out sometime during the night.

If she stayed in bed, she could simply wait for Mac to restart it or fix it, or whatever he had to do.

But what if he couldn't?

She thought of Katie. Gritting her teeth, she got out of the bed and hurried to the baby's crib. All she could make out of the baby was the shocking tuft of red hair.

Gently, she touched her cheek and was relieved to find it warm.

Shivering, she made her way to Mac's room and knocked on the door. He didn't answer.

She opened it and called, "Mac?"

Still nothing.

"Mac?" she said louder.

A loud snore was his only response.

Knowing that he had to get the house warmer before his pipes froze—before they all froze—she walked into the room toward the murky outline of his bed. She could just make out enough to navigate in the shadowed room. She reached out and shook his shoulder. His bare shoulder.

He was warm to the touch. Almost hot.

No *almost* about it—the man was hot. In a heat sort of way, not in an attractive sort of way.

Not that he wasn't attractive. He was. But that didn't mean she was attracted to him. Oh, no. The rest of the female population could *ooh* and *ahh* over Mac, but Mia would never do that. She had too much…sense. Yep, that's what she had, sense.

Of course, she didn't have enough sense to stop ogling him and wake him up already so she could crawl back into her warm bed.

"Mac," she said, "come on, wake up. There's no heat."

"What?"

"Mac, come on. I'm worried about the baby."

Reminding him of the baby worked. He sat bolt upright in bed. "What's wrong with the baby?"

"Nothing yet, but the house is cold. Very cold. Abnormally cold. You need to start up the heater or fireplace, or do something."

"You're shivering. Go get back in bed while I see what's up."

Mia knew she should argue, but she was too cold to. "Thanks. Holler if you need me."

She raced back into the guest room and scrambled back under the covers. She just wanted to go home. Or go to work. To go anywhere that wasn't here.

She'd had such odd dreams last night. Dreams that featured her and a man. A man who looked remarkably like Mac. But she was sure it wasn't Mac. After all, if she was dreaming about Mac, it would be a nightmare, not the hot kind of dream she'd experienced.

She heard a snuffling sound from the baby's crib. She got up and wrapped the quilt around her shoulders as she shuffled over to the bed.

"Hello, sleepy-head."

Katie gurgled.

"You really are a good-natured little girl, aren't you?"

Mia leaned over and retrieved the baby. "Come on, let's go downstairs and see if Mac's got a fire going. We'll change your diaper where it's warm, then get you a bottle, okay?"

She took the baby along with her blankets into her arm, and with her quilt dragging behind her, went downstairs. Mac had a roaring fire going.

"Oh, you are good," she told him as she sat down on the floor, as close as she could get to its heat. "For that, I'll even change this diaper."

"If all it takes is a fire to get out of diapers, I'd build them right into July for you."

"Ah, but I won't be here in July. As a matter of

fact, I won't be here much longer today." It was way past time to go home.

Mac got a look on his face that made her nervous.

"I won't be here much longer, will I?" she asked.

"Did you look out your window this morning?"

"No-o-o," she said slowly, dragging out the word.

"Well, remember how bad it was last night?"

"Yeah."

"It's worse today. Much worse. The power's out, which is why we had no heat. Luckily, I have a woodstove in the basement. The previous owners used it to heat the house. It's generally easier to just use the furnace, but when storms like this hit, I'm glad I have it. I got the fire up here going first. You watch Katie and I'll go start it up, okay?"

"Sure."

He left and a sinking feeling settled over Mia. She was trapped with Mac, for the foreseeable future.

Last night had been odd. Almost intimate. Sharing family stories, sharing the work of caring for the baby, of doing chores. It was almost as if they were a couple.

But the last person in the world she'd want to couple with was Larry Mackenzie.

And here she was, trapped with him.

"Great," she said to Katie. "Just great."

The baby cooed. She didn't seem to mind the weather.

Well, that made one person happy.

* * *

"Mac?" Mia asked, needing to break the silence.

She was trapped in his house, sitting next to him on his couch, because she'd tried to help him out. The least he could do was talk to her.

They'd passed the day slowly, most of their activities centered on the weather or the baby.

Mia hadn't been able to decide which required more attention, storms or babies. It was a toss-up.

Mac had got out the snowblower and tried clearing the driveway and sidewalk, but he no sooner got back inside, than everything was covered again.

Mia was pretty sure she got the best part of the workload. She'd stayed in the house with Katie, sitting close to the fire where it was warmest. She marveled at how smart the baby was.

Katie not only crawled, but sat up. Well, sometimes her sitting up seemed to involve some falling, but Mia was delighted. And Katie seemed equally impressed with her abilities. She cooed and babbled away merrily.

Mia realized that she'd quite lost her heart to Katie O'Keefe who was sleeping in Mac's arms. The warm feeling that spread through Mia's chest had to be because of Katie, not the man who cradled her so tenderly.

She had to concentrate on something other than Mac and Katie.

She tried to read, but all Mac's books seemed to

be of a legal suspense, or mystery nature. Neither of which were really holding her interest. The one in her hand was about a stalker. She just couldn't focus on the story.

That had to be why she kept glancing over at Mac. Even when he was annoying he was more interesting than the selection of reading material he kept.

The way he held Katie…it did something to her. No.

It wasn't Mac. It was his lack of a good book selection. What she wouldn't give for a good romance…something to warm her from the inside out. But Mac wasn't a romance kind of guy. The string of women Mia had watched waltz in and out of his life had more than proven that Mac would never make a commitment to any woman. But maybe he could to this baby.

"Mac," Mia repeated. "What are you going to do with Katie? You're just going to let her go?"

He obviously wasn't a talking type of guy either. She wasn't sure he was going to answer her.

He finally said, "I'm not going to *just let her go*. I'm going to find her a good home. No, not just good, the best. Perfect. People will be lining up to adopt her."

"So, you're still sure about not keeping her? I thought maybe, since you've spent some time with her, you'd have changed your mind."

If Mac kept Katie then Mia could visit her. She could baby-sit. Anytime. Why she'd—

"I'm positive I'm not keeping her. I'm not having kids—ever." His voice was flat, and there was a sense of finality about his statement.

Mia's fantasy of being the Mary Poppins baby-sitter in Katie's life evaporated. She felt a wave of sadness. "That's a shame. I've watched you with her and you'd make a good father."

"Shows how much you know," he said and then was silent.

Mia realized she'd inadvertently touched on some old wound and reached out and laid her hand on his. It was meant to be a casual, comforting touch. But there was nothing casual or comforting about it for her.

A small jolt of awareness surged through her body. She realized Mac was more than just a guy at work who drove her crazy. She felt something for him, something that went beyond their teasing, bickering relationship.

She pulled her hand back, not wanting to see more about Mac than that. She wanted to be able to go to work next week and fall back into their old comfortable rhythm of sniping and spatting. She was suddenly afraid that it wouldn't happen.

"You're seeing only a part of the picture," Mac said. "You've just seen me with Katie yesterday and today. That's nothing. Two days. Anyone can be a good parent for two days. We're talking the rest of

Katie O'Keefe's life here. And she deserves better than she'd get from me."

"And you don't think you'd always show the same care and concern for her?"

"I know I wouldn't."

"As much as I hate saying it because it would be a compliment, I'm going to say it anyway—I disagree." She smiled. "You know thinking the worst of you is my favorite pastime, but I've seen another side of you, a side you try to hide. It's not just the last couple days. It's when all those months ago you allowed yourself to be named a guardian for the child of a woman you didn't even know. It's all the time you volunteer with Our Home, helping kids who don't have anyone on their side. And now, with Katie, when you hold her, you feel something as well. Something deep. That baby couldn't ask for more. Someone who cares. Who will love her."

"You're thinking with your heart," he said, a note of derision in his tone.

It was a tone guaranteed to set Mia's teeth on edge, but this time, it didn't. She felt something else, something she wasn't going to analyze, but she was sure it wasn't annoyance.

"As a lawyer," he continued, "I have to analyze each case and work out a strategy based on all the facts at my disposal. It's not just what my client says, it's not even whether they're innocent or guilty. It's not how their story tugs at my heart. It's the whole picture."

"And are you going to share your whole story with me?"

He shook his head. "No. Just suffice to say, that there are circumstances in my past that lead me to believe that I'm not a very good risk in the parenting department. They say you emulate your parents with your own kids, and I wouldn't wish that on any child. So I've opted not to have any. Not ever. Not Katie."

She wanted to argue some more. Whatever his parents did or didn't do, whatever baggage he was carrying, she knew in her heart that it wouldn't keep him from being a good parent.

Whatever it was would make him a great one.

But she could see in his expression that he'd never believe her…couldn't believe in himself that much.

She thought she'd seen all there was to see of Mac. A strong, confident attorney. A comic who liked making people laugh. A man who had a string of women, but never let any of them get too close.

But now she saw more. She could try to tell him what she saw, but he'd never buy it, so she simply said, "Okay."

He looked surprised. "That's it? You're not going to press and pry?"

"If you ever want to tell me about whatever it is, I'll listen. That's what friends are for."

"And is that what we are? Friends?"

She smiled. "Strange as it may seem—not just strange, but shocking—I think we are. If you'd said as much last week, I'd have laughed in your face. But I've been sitting here letting the realization that something's changed between us sink in."

"Don't let it change too much," he said, serious.

"What?"

"I mean it. Friends? That I can do. But don't go falling in love with me. Even if I were looking for a relationship—which I'm not—but if I were, it wouldn't be with you. You're the kind of woman that wants the whole ball of wax. That's the last thing I want. And then there's the simple fact that we'd kill each other. So, get the stars out of your eyes. I'm not the man for you."

Mia tried—after all, men had such fragile egos—so she tried to hold back, truly she did. But she couldn't help it.

A loud chuckle escaped, just a small bark of laughter.

The baby gave a visible jump in Mac's arms, but then snuffled in closer to his chest and went back to sleep.

Mia tried to stifle the laughter, but it built and the pressure was too great. Chuckles burst out and esca-lated until she was laughing so hard that tears streamed from her eyes.

"What?" he asked in a hushed tone, looking confused.

His confusion only made her laugh harder.

"Of all the conceited—" she stopped and dragged in a long breath, trying to calm herself. "Listen, Larry, I've discovered that I do like you, which is nothing short of a miracle. But love?"

She giggled some more.

"Okay, it wasn't that funny," he said, looking annoyed.

"Sure it was. You and me? An item? In love? Why, the entire firm would never recover from the shock. We'd be able to go on *Ripley's Believe It or Not* as the world's wackiest couple. I'll admit, there's more to you than I ever imagined. I've seen that. And I'm woman enough to admit I was wrong about you. I truly believe that you'd be a great parent for Katie. But a boyfriend? A significant other? Larry, you're a real toad when it comes to women. I'm waiting for a prince and I won't settle for less."

"Frog," he said.

"What?" she asked.

Following Larry's train of thought was like jumping through flaming hoops…dangerous and more than a little scary.

"To make the analogy work, I'd have to be a frog when it came to women, not a toad."

Geesh, trust Larry to be literal. "Toad, frog…dog

for that matter. Either way, you leave a trail of women behind you. Let's agree right here and now that although our relationship may have changed a little, it's not changed enough to make me think dating you would be the wise thing to do."

"Agreed."

Katie gave a small yawn and stretched. She started blinking her eyes.

Saved by the baby, Mia thought with relief. Talking about Larry and relationships, that was just too much for any normal human being to handle.

"The snowplow just went by," Mac said. "If they've made it up here, then the main streets must be clear."

"You mean I can go home?" Mia asked, smiling broadly.

Mac felt slightly disgruntled. After all, she didn't have to look quite so happy about it.

Actually, it wasn't her look of happiness that caused his disgruntlement. The feeling had been pretty constant since her little fit of hysterics earlier.

Not that he wanted her to fall in love with him.

Mia in love with him?

It didn't bear consideration.

But still, her uncontrollable laughter at the thought was almost insulting.

A lot of women thought he was a good catch. He

was successful, ambitious and brushed his teeth regularly. Mia could do a lot worse.

But she deserved a lot better, a small voice in his head whispered.

He felt even more out-of-sorts.

"It stopped snowing almost two hours ago. The electricity is back on, and we're plowed out. Yes, I think it's time for you to go."

Mac was grateful. He'd been in Mia's company for more than twenty-four hours. That was about a day too long.

"Great! Let me run upstairs and change Katie before we bundle her up for the trip."

She scooped up the baby and practically danced up the stairs.

She didn't have to be *that* happy about leaving.

It's not as if they'd fought.

Why, they'd both been on their best behavior. No one at the firm would believe they could be together for a day and still be alive.

Of course, there was that little laughing incident. That definitely wasn't a fight. Turns out they both felt the same way. But she didn't have to laugh quite that hard.

After all, she'd been sitting there, pretending to read that book, while all the time she was making goo-goo eyes at him and the baby.

When he warned her about falling in love with

him, a small chuckle might have been warranted, but carrying on like that? Well, it was bad form.

Not that it hurt his feelings.

The last thing in the world he needed was Mia Gallagher falling in love with him.

He pressed the button on his key ring that started the car. He wanted the interior warm for Katie.

"We're ready," Mia said as she reentered the living room. "It will only take a minute to get her bundled."

"It will take more than a minute for you to get all your layers on. You start, and I'll get Katie ready."

She gave him a look—the type of look he'd grown to expect from Mia. It spoke of annoyance and aggravation.

It felt normal.

That was good, because nothing had felt normal with her since he'd picked her up yesterday.

"Come on, Katie. Let's see if I've mastered the art of bundling a baby."

He concentrated on feeding Katie's wiggling appendages into the proper openings of her snowsuit. She gurgled and seemed pleased with his attempts.

Mac purposely concentrated on Katie, and ignored Mia as she put on her multiple layers. Even with them all on she didn't look as if she'd be warm enough. She looked stiff and uncomfortable.

The woman needed a coat.

A real winter coat.

Something long, so even her knees would stay warm.

Didn't she know she lived in Erie? It was cold and snowy for at least half of the year. How could she not be prepared?

"There, we're done," he said when he clicked the car seat's last buckle into place.

"Me, too," Mia said, looking well-stuffed into her layers.

"Shall we go? The car should be warm."

"I didn't hear you go out."

"Automatic starter."

"Oh, I was just thinking about that yesterday. When I get my new car I want an automatic starter and a seat warmer. Four-wheel drive even." She gave a little wistful sigh.

Having seen Mia's jalopy, Mac hoped that new car was on the near horizon. Hers was on its last lug nut.

"Come on," he said, opening the door.

The cold arctic air hit him like a fist. He called, "Shut the door, would you," over his shoulder to Mia as he hurried to the car, wanting Katie safe and warm inside.

He'd attached the seat to the base in the car, and climbed in the front about the same time as Mia did.

"Why don't you just give me your address? Leave your car at the firm. Even though it's better out, I don't like the thoughts of you driving. I'll pick you up for work on Monday."

He expected her to argue, but she surprised him by saying, "Taking me straight home is a great idea, but don't worry about picking me up. I'm on Donovan's way. I'll give him a call."

"Fine," he said.

Of course, it was fine. Going to collect Mia on Monday would be out of his way. He was going to have to deal with getting the baby ready and didn't need one more thing to do on his morning list.

Yes, that was fine.

But that same odd feeling swept over him.

Mac was thankful that the roads still required a great deal of concentration. It didn't leave time for small talk. He was pretty sure he and Mia had had enough of that to last them months.

He drove to her apartment building and put the car in Park. "Thanks again. I don't know what I'd have done without you."

She gave him a small smile. "You're welcome. I hate to say this, but truly, it was my pleasure."

"I…" he forgot what he wanted to say. The words just faded as he looked at Mia smiling. It was dazzling, robbing him of the ability to put a coherent string of words together. Making him want to—

Before he knew it, he'd leaned over and was kissing her. A soft, tender kiss, inviting her to claim more, but not insisting.

A kiss that waited, willing to break off, but hoping for so much more.

Mia's lips softened, sinking into his, lingering, tasting.

It was Mac who broke it off, pulling back.

"Um, thanks," he said.

Mia sat there a moment, looking dazed. A look of shock quickly replaced it. A faint pink hue crept into her cheeks.

"You're welcome. Goodbye," she called as she opened the door, and fled, slamming it in her wake.

Mac watched her run into the small, run-down apartment building.

What the hell had he just done?

Three hours later, he still hadn't figured out what on earth had possessed him to kiss Amelia Gallagher.

Katie was napping. He'd put her in the crib and had the monitor volume cranked to the highest setting. He could hear each soft inhale and exhale.

Listening to Katie breathe he tried to think of something other than Mia and the kiss.

THE KISS.

He'd started thinking of it all in capitals.

Kissing Mia. Who would have thought?

That small kiss had left him wanting more…more than kisses. He wanted—

The phone rang, interrupting his highly inappropriate fantasy.

"Hello?" Maybe it was Mia. Maybe she couldn't stop thinking about the kiss either.

"Hi, honey," Mrs. Z. said, her voice cheery.

Not Mia. Of course it wasn't Mia. He was sure she'd forgotten all about him the moment he pulled away from her building.

"Hi," he said. "What's up?"

"I just called to see how you made out in the storm. We've got about three inches here, so driving's a mess. But hopefully it will all be cleared by Monday."

"Things here are…well, interesting at the moment, and it doesn't have anything to do with the storm pretty much closing down the city."

"Interesting how?"

"Well…" he launched into the story of how he'd come to have a baby, about Mia's help. He left out the kiss, but stuck to the rest of the story, including the fact that he needed to find a home for Katie. Mrs. Z. just listened.

Listening was one of the things Kelley Zumigala did best.

"Well, I'd say you've been busy," she said with a chuckle.

"Do you think you'd help me?"

He hated to ask for help. It had galled him to have to ask Mia. It was a bit easier to ask Mrs. Z. He knew she'd say yes, that she'd do whatever she could for him.

"What do you need, honey?"

"Maybe an opinion, when I narrow down some potential parents for Katie?"

"You know I always have an opinion and sharing them is a pleasure, much to Chet and Sal's dismay."

He laughed.

They all bristled under the weight of Mrs. Z.'s opinions on occasion, but truth be told, he'd never known her to be wrong.

"Thanks, I knew I could count on you."

"Now, about this Mia?" There was a hint of plotting in her tone. She was always trying to find him a girlfriend.

"No way, Mrs. Z. If you saw us together you'd know that there's absolutely no way Mia and I could ever have a relationship."

He wasn't going to tell her about the kiss.

It didn't mean anything.

He'd kissed women before, and would again. Although at the moment, the only woman he wanted to kiss was Mia. And that was plain crazy.

"I didn't say a word about a relationship," Mrs. Z. said. "Not a word."

And Mac wasn't going to say a word about that

kiss. He wasn't going to think about, wasn't going to speak about it. It was a freak incident brought on by too much stress.

And he was over it.

He had a baby to worry about. Why he'd probably forget all about THE KISS tomorrow.

"I'll call you next week," he said.

"Sure. I'm anxious to hear what else you have to say about this Mia."

Nothing, Mac thought as he hung up.

He wouldn't have anything else to say about her.

He was done thinking about her…about her and THE KISS.

Chapter Five

"Mia," Mac yelled, as he rushed into the office Monday morning.

He didn't bang the snow off his boots again, but this time Mia hardly noticed. Her attention was focused on the car seat in his hands.

She'd missed the baby yesterday and worried how Mac was doing with her on his own.

She'd wanted to call and check on them both—had picked up the phone at least a dozen times, but each time she'd replaced the receiver, the call unmade. She felt awkward…almost shy.

She'd always had a lot of feelings regarding Mac. Anger, annoyance, frustration…but not shyness.

In one weekend their relationship had shifted. Not just because she'd really spent time with him.

Their relationship had altered because Mac had kissed her.

She spent Sunday trying to busy herself around her apartment: doing laundry, talking to her brothers, cleaning…but whatever she did, whoever she spoke to, her thoughts kept circling back to one fact, Mac had kissed her.

And she'd kissed him back.

That was the most disturbing part, the *kissed- him- back* part.

What on earth had she been thinking?

She hadn't been thinking, that was the problem.

Being with Mac for almost twenty-four continuous hours had obviously fried her brain. That was the only explanation she could come up with. Otherwise she would never have kissed him back.

Never.

Now she'd had a full Mac-free day and her mind was working fine and she realized the kiss meant nothing, but still she felt odd as he rushed in with Katie in her seat.

Mia didn't like it and decided she'd ignore it.

Yeah, she'd ignore feeling shy, just like she planned to ignore the fact he'd kissed her. And she especially planned to ignore the fact she'd kissed him back.

She forced a smile—a non-shy-smile—and said, "Hi, Mac," then kicked herself for forgetting to call him Larry.

He didn't seem to notice as he said, in a rush, "I'd arranged for Leland's daughter Brigitta to take care of Katie today while I was at court, but she called this morning and said her kids are all down with the flu, and I don't want to take the chance of Katie getting sick, so…"

He paused, letting the question hang unasked.

Mia could have forced him to actually make the request, but instead said, "I'll watch her. I missed her yesterday."

"You don't mind?" He sounded surprised.

"Of course not. Katie and I are buddies. I'm doing it for her," she added as an afterthought. The last thing she wanted was for Mac to think she was doing it for him.

"And you know Mr. Wagner," she continued, "he's all about family. Given the special circumstances, he won't mind her visiting the office today."

"What won't I mind?" Leland Wagner asked, as he came out of his office. He was a man who wore his years with ease and grace. Gray hair and a ready smile. He was the reason the firm felt more like an extended family than a business.

Leland Wagner was the heart of Wagner, Mc-Duffy, Chambers and Donovan.

"You won't mind if I watch Mac's baby while he's at court, right?" Mia asked.

"Not *my* baby," Mac said, sounding horrified at the very idea.

"Don't get nervous, Mac," Leland said with a chuckle. "I talked to Brigitta this morning and she told me the whole story. She feels awful about letting you down. She also told me about what you're going to do for the baby. Of course I don't mind. You know that we believe in family here. And what could be more family than a baby? She's welcome to visit until you can make other arrangements for her."

"Thanks," Mac told Mr. Wagner, before turning to Mia. "Listen, all her stuff's in the diaper bag. You know the drill as well as I do."

He glanced at his watch. "I've really got to run, or I'm going to be late."

"Go," she said, taking the car seat from him. "I think after this weekend, I can handle anything."

"Thanks, you're the best." With that, he flew out of the office.

"This weekend?" Mr. Wagner asked, after Mac had raced out of the office. "Brigitta didn't say anything about this weekend being significant to you and Mac."

"Oh, it was nothing. Certainly nothing of significance," Mia assured her boss, feeling her face warm.

There was no way anyone could know about

Mac's kiss, but still, she didn't want to talk about any of their time together.

She busied herself getting Katie out of her car seat and tried not to notice the speculative way Mr. Wagner was studying her.

"I just helped out with Katie a bit this weekend," she added, hoping that would end Mr. Wagner's inquiry.

"You helped out Mac? On purpose? And you both survived?" Mr. Wagner laughed, then murmured, "Well, will wonders never cease."

"Come on, Mac and I aren't that bad, are we?"

"The two of you are an office legend. The way you fight and carry on. There's generally only two reasons why people are at odds like that." He waited a beat and when she didn't respond he said, "Aren't you going to ask what they are?"

"No." She had Katie unbuckled, and began unzipping her snowsuit. "But I bet you're going to tell me anyway."

"Of course. That's one of the perks of being senior partner...of just being a senior. You get to talk and everyone else has to listen. Now, as I was saying, there's generally only two reasons why two people behave the way you two do. Either they don't like each other—"

"Yep, that's the one." Mia lifted the de-coated baby and kissed her forehead. "Hey, you."

Katie smiled and gurgled happily.

"—or…" he said slowly.

Mia looked from Katie to her boss. Mr. Wagner was grinning.

"Or, they *do* like each other, but don't want to admit it. So they spend their days haranguing each other to try to cover the attraction."

"There's no covering of attraction between Mac and me. We are definitely the first one. We don't like each other. But it just so happens we both do like Katie," she punctuated the statement by giving the baby another kiss on the forehead. "So we've called a truce."

That's what Mac's kiss had been, a mark of truce. Nothing more. Which didn't quite explain why it had featured prominently in her dreams. But Mia wasn't going to question the reason, to dig any deeper.

The kiss was a truce. A symbol of their unity. Nothing more or less.

"If you say so," Mr. Wagner said, his tone implying that he didn't quite believe her. But he didn't press. Instead he cooed at Katie. "Oh, isn't she a beauty. What's her name again?"

"Katie. Katie O'Keefe."

Mia gave the baby a tiny squeeze. How on earth was Mac ever going to let her go? If Katie were hers, Mia could never give her up.

"Katie Cupcakes," Mr. Wagner practically cooed, "would you like to come see Grandpa Wagner?"

He held out his arms and Mia handed the baby over.

"Be careful," she warned. "She squirms. She also crawls and is getting pretty good at the whole sitting-up thing. Although she's better at the falling-down part."

"I'm an expert at babies," he said.

Leland Wagner looked like an expert, holding the baby on his hip, chucking her chin with his free hand. "She can squirm all she wants and I won't drop her."

"Okay," Mia said, still watching him like a hawk.

"How about I take her around the office to meet everyone?"

"Really, she's fine with me. I don't want to put you out. You're being so nice to let me keep her at all."

"That's not it, you're nervous I'll drop her. Nervous about letting her out of your sight. Don't worry, I won't take offense. All my girls were the same way when they had their babies. Overprotective. They forgot I raised them all right. But never fear. I promise, I'll bring her back shortly, safe and sound."

There was nothing Mia could say after that. She smiled and nodded, but couldn't help feeling anxious as he walked up the stairs with the baby.

It was ridiculous. Mr. Wagner had far more experience with babies than she did.

Katie was fine.

But still, a sense of unease settled in the pit of Mia's stomach. It had to be that she was anxious about the baby. After all, it wasn't as if she had anything else to be anxious about.

A mental image of Mac flitted through her mind, but she blocked it out quite firmly.

Mr. Wagner was wrong. She didn't feel anything at all for Mac, except a bond of common goals because of their mutual affection for the baby.

That was all.

Nothing more.

Nothing less.

But even as she thought it, she wasn't quite sure she believed it.

Mac had to force himself to concentrate on the hearing, his thoughts kept drifting back to Mia and the baby. He called during both breaks to check on them.

His excuse was Katie, but in reality, he just wanted to talk to Mia. He'd wanted to call her all day yesterday, but didn't have any excuse then.

He wasn't sure why he had this sudden need to talk to Mia, to be with her.

All he knew was that the house had seemed empty without her. Much to his surprise, he handled Katie's care just fine. As a matter of fact, the baby was a delight. Filling the house with laughter and gurgles.

Even when Katie was sleeping there was the gentle sound of her breathing over the monitor.

She made the house finally feel lived-in.

Mac had bought the Glenwood house five years ago. It had been a comfortable place to live, but suddenly it was more than just a place. With the baby there it had somehow come alive.

And it wasn't just Katie.

Somehow during her short visit, Mia had left an impression on the house. Warming it, altering it. He'd missed that on Sunday.

At four-thirty he finally left the courthouse and walked the few short, cold blocks back to the firm. Back to Mia and Katie. His heart felt unbelievably light.

"Hey, how're my girls?" he asked as he walked into the office.

"Shh," Mia said as she nodded behind the elaborate antique desk that Sarah Donovan had installed when she remodeled the office. "She fell asleep about an hour ago. She was totally exhausted. You can blame Mr. Wagner. He spent the better part of the afternoon showing her off, visiting everyone in the office."

Mac laughed. "She was okay then?"

"Like I told you both times you called, she was more than okay. Katie was great. She's got to be one of the most laid-back babies ever. She helped me greet clients as they came in. Everyone's fallen in love with her."

The clients weren't the only ones who'd fallen in love with the baby. Mia had lost her heart to Katie

O'Keefe. She didn't say it, but Mac could see the emotion in her eyes.

She was head-over-heels in love with the baby. It was there in the softness that crept into her voice every time she said Katie's name.

For a moment he had a fleeting desire to hear her say his name with the same sort of softness, instead of the annoyance that generally accented his name from her lips.

"Still," he said, "I can't thank you enough. And I'd like to make it up to you."

"How?" Mia asked.

"Come have dinner with Katie and me. She missed you last night."

"Larry, I don't know," she sounded uncertain.

His name wasn't quite tinged with the same softness she said Katie with, but it wasn't infused with her normal dose of annoyance. Just confusion.

That was good, because Mac was confused as hell himself. Between work and Katie, he didn't have time to try and figure out what was disturbing him.

All he knew was he wanted to spend the evening with Mia. The feeling went almost beyond want into a more intense territory. He needed to spend time with her.

He wasn't going to analyze or weigh the need. It was just there. He was going to accept it.

Mia was still silent.

"Do you have a date?" he asked, an unfamiliar twisting in his gut as he asked.

"No."

Mac let out a breath he hadn't realized he was holding at her answer.

He smiled as he asked, "Some prior commitment then? A dinner with some Hollywood boy-toy…I wouldn't mind coming second-fiddle to something like that."

She grinned then said, "No. No Hollywood boy-toys this week. But I'm sure one will be calling any time now."

Mac laughed. "So you like boy-toys?"

"To be honest, I like real men, not boys…toys or otherwise."

Mac grinned. "I don't think I qualify as boyish, and I know it's not that I intimidate you. Other people maybe, but never you. And I know you adore Katie. So, why would you pass up a free dinner? Pizza, with everything."

Her smile evaporated.

"The kiss," she said softly.

"What kiss?" Mac said, feigning confusion.

Truth be told, that kiss was all he'd thought about after dropping her off.

Why had he kissed Mia Gallagher?

He didn't like her. She was a constant thorn in his side. The reason he was inviting her out tonight—the reason she'd been on his mind so much—must be that he owed her big for all her help with Katie. First this weekend, now today.

Yeah, that must be why.

"Gratitude," he said. "It was just a small thank-you gesture. Nothing more, nothing less."

"So, you thank every woman who helps you by sticking your tongue down her throat?" she asked.

There was a hint of the old Mia, the one who was never afraid to call him on the carpet, in that tone.

"It was little more than a peck. Come on, Mia, it was just a small kiss. If I ever really kiss you, you'll know it."

"Kiss?" Donovan said, as he walked into the entryway.

Mia jumped, as if caught in a compromising situation.

"Who's kissing whom?" Donovan asked.

"Me," she said hurriedly. "Kissing Katie. Larry here's afraid I'll give her germs."

"I may not be a baby expert," Donovan said, "but I think Katie will survive a few germs. At least I hope so. I think half the office kissed her at one time or another today."

Germs?

Mac hadn't thought about germs. What would happen if Katie got sick?

His stomach clenched.

Get FREE BOOKS and a FREE GIFT when you play the...

LAS VEGAS
GAME

Just scratch off
the gold box with a coin.
Then check below to see
the gifts you get!

YES! I have scratched off the gold Box. Please send me my **2 FREE BOOKS** and **gift for which I qualify.** I understand that I am under no obligation to purchase any books as explained on the back of this card.

310 SDL DZ9Q   210 SDL DZ95

FIRST NAME	LAST NAME

ADDRESS

APT.#	CITY

(S-R-08/04)

STATE/PROV.   ZIP/POSTAL CODE

7	7	7	Worth TWO FREE BOOKS plus a BONUS Mystery Gift!
🍒	🍒	🍒	Worth TWO FREE BOOKS!
🔔	🔔	♣	TRY AGAIN!

www.eHarlequin.com

Offer limited to one per household and not valid to current Silhouette Romance® subscribers. All orders subject to approval.

BUSINESS REPLY MAIL
FIRST-CLASS MAIL   PERMIT NO. 717-003   BUFFALO, NY

POSTAGE WILL BE PAID BY ADDRESSEE

SILHOUETTE READER SERVICE
3010 WALDEN AVE
PO BOX 1867
BUFFALO NY 14240-9952

NO POSTAGE
NECESSARY
IF MAILED
IN THE
UNITED STATES

"Maybe I better make an appointment with a pediatrician, just in case," he said. "I can't believe I didn't think of it sooner. She should be checked out. What if something's wrong with her and we don't know it?"

"Mac, she looks pretty healthy to me," Mia said soothingly.

"Looks can be deceiving. Maybe I should call Brigitta. Her kids are sick, which means she must know a good doctor. Do you think they'd get me in tonight?"

"It's awfully late," Donovan said.

"Or, there's Louisa at The Chocolate Bar, her husband's a doctor," Mia offered. "He works at the E.R. and probably sees a ton of kids there. Bet we could ask him to stop over and take a look at her. Want me to call? I'd feel better getting her a clean bill of health, although I still maintain babies need kisses, germs or no germs."

Mac could see she wanted the baby checked out as much as he did. But he also noticed she was still sticking to the kissing-baby cover story in hopes Donovan didn't catch onto the fact she'd been kissing him.

And Mac had been kissing her.

He still wasn't sure why, but he was sure he'd very much like to kiss Mia Gallagher again.

But first they had to see to Katie.

"Yes, why don't you call him and see if Joe will come give Katie a once-over. Call him, okay?"

"I'll do it now," Mia said, already pulling out the phone book.

"Can Katie stay here while I run up to my office?" Mac asked.

"Sure. Oh, you had a delivery. I put it on your desk."

It had come. He couldn't resist a smile at the thought.

"Thanks," he said. He hurried up the stairs to his office and realized they never settled the dinner discussion. Damn.

Donovan caught up to him at the top of the stairs. "So, you kissed Mia, huh?"

Mac turned to him sharply. "What on earth makes you say that?"

Donovan didn't reply, just stared at him, waiting for an answer.

Mac sighed. "Yeah, I kissed her. I don't know why she's making so much of it. You either. It was just a thank-you for all the help she gave me this weekend. I don't know what I would have done without her then, or today for that matter."

And since he'd started a tradition of kissing Mia as thanks, he probably owed her another kiss for her help today.

It was a pleasant thought. It shouldn't be, but it was.

"So, you kiss everyone you thank?" Donovan

asked. "I helped you out on that Roger's case and you never kissed me."

He chuckled as he puckered his lips.

Mac slugged him lightly on the arm. "And you can be sure I'm never going to."

"Sarah will be relieved." Donovan stopped laughing and asked, "So, are you going to kiss her again?"

"The baby?" Mac asked.

"Amelia."

"Mia," Mac corrected. "She's going by Mia now. And Mia obviously takes a small peck on the cheek way too seriously," he tried to explain, not really answering Donovan's question. After all, he'd just been thinking about kissing Mia as a thank-you for today's help.

"That's all it was, a small peck on the cheek? That's not what it sounded like to me."

"Okay so it wasn't her cheek, but it wasn't serious," Mac maintained. "Hell, if I ever seriously kiss her, she'll know."

"Okay," Donovan said as he started down the hall toward his office.

Mac walked into his and spotted the box on his desk.

He opened it and smiled.

Perfect.

Just what he wanted.

Dinner with Mac.

On purpose.

Mia figured she must be out of her mind.

She tried to convince herself she'd only said yes because she was hungry. Mac had ordered a pepperoni and mushroom pizza from Teresa's, one of her favorite delis.

"Pizza beats cooking any day of the week," Mia said as she finished her second slice. She glanced at the baby, sleeping in her car seat and wondered how mean it would be to nudge the seat and wake her up.

Things seemed…more awkward without Katie running interference. After all, there's no way Mia would be sitting in Mac's kitchen having dinner with him if it wasn't for the baby.

Mac must have felt it too because he looked as if he felt as awkward as she felt.

"So, did you make any calls about finding a family for Katie?"

"No," he said. "I was tied up at court all day."

"I thought maybe you'd done some checking during a break."

"No. I called you during breaks."

"To check on the baby," she hurriedly clarified.

"Yeah. Checking on Katie. There would be no other reason to call you."

"Right," she said. "We don't have a call-you-on-the-phone sort of relationship."

"Yes. What we have is a…partnership. We're working together for Katie's sake."

"Yes," Mia said with relief that they'd clarified what they had. "The baby. Nothing else."

They lapsed into an awkward silence as they finished the pizza.

Katie still slept, blissfully unaware of the tension that radiated between the adults.

"I have to go get something from the car," Mac said abruptly as he finished his dinner.

"No problem," she said, relieved for a brief respite. "I'll clean this up. Maybe Katie will wake up and I can help with her bath before I go home."

She busied herself around the kitchen, making herself at home. She was just wiping off the table when Mac came in carrying a large box.

"Here," he said, thrusting it at her and looking uncomfortable. "This is for you."

"For me?"

"I wanted to do something to thank you for jumping in and helping me with the baby. You didn't have to, but you did. Not just over the weekend, but today."

She just stood there gaping. "You didn't have to…I mean…"

"Just open it. I called Sarah and she said this should be okay, size-wise."

Mia set the box down on the table and opened it slowly. It was black…a coat. She pulled it from the box. A long, wool coat. Soft. Thick. Definitely warmer—much warmer—than her old one.

"Listen," he said, "I know you. You're going to get all huffy, especially since I made cracks about your layered look. But I didn't mean buying the coat as an insult. I just knew it was something you could use and I wanted to thank you and," he paused and then said, "sale. It was on sale, so—"

"Mac, I'm not going to get mad. This was—" she paused, stroking one hand down the fabric "—it was kind and thoughtful. Those are two words I never thought I'd use to describe you, but I guess I've discovered there's a lot about you I didn't know."

"So, are you going to just stand there holding it, or are you going to try it on?" he asked, his voice gruff, his expression flustered, as if he didn't know what to make of her compliment.

Mia hoped he didn't, because she didn't know what to make of it…what to make of all the new things she was learning about Mac.

"If it's not the right size the clerk said you can exchange it, but like I said, I called Sarah and she said it should work."

He took it from her hand and held it out for her to slip on.

Mia slipped her arms through the sleeves. The coat fit perfectly. And fell to her knees.

"It's beautiful," she said.

"I wasn't going for beautiful. I was going for warm."

"Well, it's both. You didn't have to, but thank

you." She leaned up and before she knew what she was doing, she'd kissed his cheek.

Now she was the one who felt as flustered as he had looked.

She started to back away, but Mac stopped her, wrapping his arms around her and pulling her close.

"You're welcome," he said, his voice soft and low. "Mia, I—"

She didn't let him finish. She knew what he wanted, and though she wasn't sure why, she wanted it as well, so she moved forward and kissed him again. Not on his cheek, but firmly on his lips.

She meant it to be a quick kiss, just enough to shake this odd longing from her system. But quick wasn't in the cards.

The kiss lingered, then deepened.

Mac's arms tightened around her, pulling her close. And suddenly the coat was too much of a barrier.

Anything that separated her from him was too much. She wanted to be closer, to feel the heat of his body radiate into hers. She wanted to absorb it, to hold it.

She wanted—

The doorbell rang and she backed away, feeling stunned.

Mac swore. "Who could that be?"

It took a moment for her to order her thoughts.

"Maybe Joe? He was supposed to stop, remember?" Her voice sounded breathless, as if she'd just run a race.

"Well, let me just say, he has crappy timing," Mac grumbled as he released her.

Mia stepped away, putting distance between them. "Or maybe good timing. I don't know what we were doing."

The bell rang again and Katie stirred, looked around and started to fuss.

"Remind me and I'll give you an explanation of just what we were doing and what it might have led to later."

Mia slid off the coat, running her hand across the soft fabric one more time before she hurried to get the baby.

She wasn't about to ask for the explanation Mac had offered. She wouldn't need it because she wasn't about to kiss him again. She had plans, a future. And though kissing Mac might be a pleasant diversion, she knew there was no future in it.

She knew she shouldn't allow it to happen again.

She knew there was nothing she wanted more.

Chapter Six

It wasn't just Joe Delacamp at the door. The new E.R. doctor, had brought his wife.

Louisa Delacamp was rather new to the Square as well. She owned The Chocolate Bar, a sweet shop. Louisa herself had a sweetness about her that had nothing to do with the chocolate she sold and everything to do with her true nature.

The Square had adopted her as one of their own from the day she moved onto it.

The dark-haired doctor and his redheaded wife radiated the same type of happiness Donovan and Sarah, and Josh Gardner and his wife Libby did.

It was enough to make a confirmed bachelor like

Mac cower in his boots. But Mac knew there was no way he would ever fall victim to the marriage curse. He was immune.

"I heard the word baby and invited myself," Louisa said as she brushed passed Mac and made a beeline toward Mia and Katie.

"Amelia?" she said. "I'm surprised to see you here."

"Mia," Mac corrected Louisa.

He smiled as he said her name. Yes, she was definitely more a Mia than an Amelia. He wondered how he'd missed that before. Maybe he'd been too busy annoying her to notice her true nature. But he noticed now.

She gave him a look—one that Mac had no trouble reading as a *butt-out* look.

"Hi, Louisa," Mia said. "I'm just here…helping out. You know men, they can be clueless when it comes to babies. And since Mac is habitually clueless, you can imagine how much I worry about him alone with Katie."

Mac should have been insulted. After all, he'd handled Katie's care as well as Mia had. But instead, he grinned at her, which made her scowl.

She was trying to reestablish their old trading-barbs relationship. He suspected it was a defense mechanism. Why would she feel the need to be defensive?

THE KISS.

Not just one kiss anymore, he reminded himself. Kisses.

He'd exchanged kiss*es* with Mia, and the idea of multiple kisses bothered her so much that she was going on the defensive.

He smiled even broader and she scowled even harder.

"Hey, you two," Joe said. "Donovan's not here to call a time-out, so I guess it's up to me. I can't imagine how the two of you manage without a referee."

"I just bet you can't imagine how we manage it," Mac said. "Want me to tell you?"

"No," Mia said hastily. "Joe doesn't want to hear about our tempestuous relationship. He's here to do us a favor and check out Katie."

"May I hold her?" Louisa asked.

"Sure," Mia said, handing the wriggling baby over to Louisa.

"Isn't she precious. I hope ours is a girl," she murmured to Joe.

"Yours?" Mia asked. "Is there something you want to share?"

Louisa had slipped quietly into the rhythm of the Square, never making waves, as she seamlessly fit herself, her son and her surrogate father, Elmer, into the fabric of the neighborhood.

But last year, she hadn't just made waves, she'd created a tsunami when Joe Delacamp came back into her life to reclaim a son he never knew he had…and soon thereafter reclaimed Louisa, too.

"Well," Louisa said slowly, looking to Joe who smiled and nodded. "We haven't told anyone yet, but we're going to have a baby. I'm only a couple months along." Her hand drifted to her still flat stomach. She caressed it gently.

"Aaron is beside himself with excitement," Joe blurted. "He can't wait to be a big brother."

"Congratulations," Mia said, hugging Louisa, catching Katie up in between them.

"Congratulations," Mac told Joe as he slapped him on the back. "How are you handling it?"

"Scared to death," Joe said. "I never planned on having kids, never imagined the possibility. But then I found out about Aaron and now, with this baby? I'm sure you know how it can be overwhelming and yet, invigorating, what with having Katie."

"No," Mac said. "Not the same thing at all. Katie's not really mine, just temporarily my responsibility. It's not the same thing as having one of your own."

Mac saw Mia give him a sad look as he said the words.

The same look she gave him every time he mentioned finding Katie a real family.

He hated that look.

He preferred having Mia bluster and trade barbs with him. That sad, resigned look left him feeling as if he'd disappointed her. But she had no call to have expectations about him, which meant there was no way he could disappoint her.

Suddenly all business, Joe said, "So, let's do a quick checkup then."

In short order Joe had proclaimed Katie a healthy, happy baby.

Mac felt relief flood through his system. He hadn't realized he was that worried there was something wrong with her.

"You'll need to find out if she's up-to-date on her immunizations."

"From what I know about her mother, I'm sure she was." Even if Marion had had to do without something, she'd have seen to it.

"And you'll have to find a pediatrician for her," Joe said. "I've worked with Mavis Samuels at the hospital. She's a good doctor and is great with the kids."

"I'll call her next week," Mac said.

"Can I get you something to drink?" Mia asked.

"No, but thanks," Louisa said. "As much as I'd like to stay and play with Katie some more, I'd better get back. Elmer's watching Aaron, but he has a hot date later."

"Is he still seeing Mabel?" Mia asked.

Mabel was the Square's acupuncturist, and she and Elmer were the latest Perry Square romance news.

It amazed Mac how small town-like the Square

felt. After all, Erie might not be New York City, but it was a city…a city that seemed to disappear on the Square, which lay in the heart of Erie's downtown.

On Perry Square everyone knew everyone's business, and no one hesitated to offer advice and opinions.

He shook his head.

"Yes, Mabel and Elmer are still dating," Louisa said with a happy little sigh. "They're so cute together. And I've never seen him like this. That's what a good relationship can do for you…make you happy."

Mac felt as uncomfortable at that statement as Mia looked. After all, they didn't have a relationship. They had a couple kisses. Nothing more.

"I'm happy for them," Mia said.

"Me, too," Louisa stood and passed Katie back to Mia. "Elmer deserves finding someone who makes him happy…everyone does."

Louisa gave her husband a look. One of those couple-speak looks Mac had seen the Zumigalas use over the years. It made him feel even more uncomfortable.

Louisa looked away from her husband and added, "Thanks for letting me get a baby fix."

"Anytime. And congratulations, again," Mia said.

"Thanks," Louisa said.

Mac had heard the expression about pregnant women glowing, but he'd never given it much thought until now. Louisa was positively beaming as she continued, "It's like a dream come true. Having Joe back in my life, being a family. Everything seems so perfect that sometimes it almost scares me."

"A good kind of scary?" Mia asked.

"The best. I love The Chocolate Bar, love that it's doing well. But without Joe and Aaron, and now this new baby, it wouldn't mean anything. Love. Family. They're what make life sweet."

Mia was still mulling over Louisa's statement the next morning.

After Joe and Louisa had left, she'd helped put Katie to bed, then made a quick escape.

She didn't want to be alone with Mac. She needed distance, time to think about what was going on between them. About what it meant.

And yet, leaving had been hard. She'd wanted to stay and just talk to him, as much as she'd wanted to leave.

The conflicting desires didn't make sense.

And a restless night's sleep didn't make figuring things out any easier. She felt decidedly unrested and out of sorts when she arrived at the office the next morning.

The door was still locked, which meant she was the first one there. Good. She'd have a few moments to try to gather her rather frazzled wits. There'd be a few precious minutes to herself before the day kicked into high gear.

She unlocked the front door and let herself into the quiet office. She took off her coat—the new coat Mac had given her. It was such a thoughtful gift. She probably should have protested that it was too expensive, too extravagant.

She was hanging it in the closet when the door burst open. For a moment, Mia's heart rate picked up speed, thinking it was Mac and Katie.

But it settled right back into place when she saw that it wasn't. It was Pearly Gates, the self-proclaimed busybody of Perry Square.

"Now, I'm hearing rumors flying," Pearly said with a faint touch of the South in her voice and no preamble at all, "and you know me, I hate rumors…unless I happen to be the one spreadin' them. No beating around the bush here. What's going on between you and Mac? And what's this about him having a baby."

The older woman took a seat next to Mia's desk and waited expectantly for an answer.

Mia followed and took her own seat, knowing there was no way out of offering up some explanation. Pearly was as tenacious as a bloodhound when she was on the scent of a story. She wouldn't let go until she was satisfied she had all the news.

"Nothing to the first part," Mia said. "There's nothing between Mac and I," *except a few kisses she wasn't going to mention,* "and he doesn't really have a baby to answer the second part of your question."

"You answered my questions, but left me with more, so spill it. Not some short little explanation you hope will satisfy me. It won't. I want the whole scoop."

Sighing, Mia began telling Pearly everything. Everything except the kisses. "…and the snow finally let up and Mac took me home. He's looking for an adoptive family for Katie. Until he finds one, he's taking care of her."

"Mac?" Pearly asked, picking up on Mia's slip.

"Larry," Mia corrected. "I'm helping Larry."

"Helping Larry Mackenzie?" Pearly shook her head. "I never would have believed it if I hadn't heard it from your own lips."

"Me either," Mia confessed. "But I feel better assuring myself that I'm not really helping Mac, I'm helping with Katie. There's a difference. One's big, annoying and hard to like, one's small, cute and ever so easy to love."

"You called him Mac again," Pearly—obviously in her bloodhound mode—persisted.

"What?" Mia asked, though she'd heard Pearly just fine.

"I've never heard you call Larry Mackenzie *Mac* before today. And now you've done it twice in one conversation. Everyone else on the Square calls him Mac, but not you."

Darn.

Mia shrugged and tried to play nonchalant. "I just slipped. He's not as annoying when he's not here, so sometimes I forget to call him Larry, at least when he's absent."

"It wasn't just that you called him Mac," Pearly said, speculation in her look. "It's that you said his name with a certain softness in your voice. The kind of nuance that only comes when a woman's been kissing a man."

"Pearly. You know I'd rather kiss a toad…" *Frog,* Mia mentally corrected, a small smile playing on her lips. Like Mac had said, the analogy required a frog, not a toad. "…than kiss Larry Mackenzie."

"You might rather, but you didn't kiss a toad. You kissed Mac."

"I did not."

Mia crossed her fingers as she made the denial, even though she was telling the truth.

She hadn't kissed Mac.

He'd kissed her.

There was a difference.

A big difference.

And the second time they kissed didn't count.

"Have I ever told you about the time I was the belle of the county fair?" Pearly asked, changing the subject.

Mia was happy to switch the topic of conversation to something else. The more she denied kissing with Mac, the more likely she was to slip up and admit the truth.

"No," she said. "I've heard a lot of your stories, but I don't think I've heard one about being belle of the county fair."

"Well, my class had a kissing booth at the fair to raise money for our trip to Atlanta. And oh, what a trip that was, why—"

"The kissing booth?" Mia prompted, trying to get the older lady back on track.

Pearly had a habit of veering off onto conversational tangents. Since her stories were hard enough to follow when they were linear, most of the Square had learned to try to keep her from diverging.

"Right, the kissing booth. Well, I didn't plan on working it, but a friend, Shirley was her name, volunteered me to take a turn. I kissed a hundred boys that weekend. But there was one boy, Buster McClinnon…he was different. Buster was the first boy I ever kissed. But we hadn't done much kissing of late. We fought a lot, Buster and I. But the moment his lips hit mine, *pow*. It hit me hard and I forgot all about our current fight."

Pearly drifted a moment. Her gaze had a faraway quality about it, and Mia knew the older woman had slipped into the past, to a time when she fought and kissed one Buster McClinnon.

All of a sudden, Pearly returned to the here-and-now and started right back into her story, "Afterward, I tried to figure out what made the touch of his lips so much different than all those other boys."

"Did you figure it out?" Mia asked.

"When I talked to Shirley, she had an answer. She said there are all kinds of kisses. There are kisses you share with family, there are kisses you share with friends. Kissing booth kisses are an entirely different breed of kiss…not really a kiss at all. Just two sets of lips touching."

Pearly paused and got a far away look in her eyes again. "And then, there are the ones that matter. The kisses that people can see on your face, can hear in your voice. That's the kind of kiss you gave Mac. It's the kind of kiss I gave Buster. It's special. It means something."

"Kissing Mac doesn't mean anything. It's not special."

"Ah ha," Pearly crowed with glee. "You admit you kissed him."

Darn.

Now that Pearly Gates, aka The Perry Square town crier, knew Mia had been kissing Mac, the news would be all over the Square before dinner.

Heck, knowing the speed that the Perry Square gossip-mongers moved at, it would be all over the Square by lunch.

"Who are you, Perry Mason?" Mia grumbled.

"Evading the question," Pearly declared, looking triumphant. "The guilty tend to try that sort of thing."

"I'm not guilty," Mia protested.

"Never said you were. And if you are, you shouldn't be. You and Mac would make a perfect couple. You…" she said, pausing, searching for a word, "…balance. Yeah. You balance each other."

"I don't want to balance with anyone, especially not *Larry* Mackenzie."

She purposefully added an extra umph to Larry's name to prove that despite her slips, she thought of Mac as Larry. "I have plans. Plans that go beyond a car with leather seat-warmer seats. I'm going back to school."

Before Mac and Katie's concerns had taken over her thoughts, Mia had been desperately trying to decide what to do next. Where she wanted her life to go.

Saying the words I'm-going-back-to-school aloud to Pearly solidified the thought. It made sense. It felt right.

She rummaged through a pile of papers and found the brochure from Mercyhurst. "Yes, I'm going back to school and finishing my degree. I quit so I could help my brothers through school. But now that Ryan's graduating, it's time to go back."

"Good for you." Pearly seemed genuinely happy at Mia's pronouncement.

"That means, I can't get involved with anyone," Mia said slowly.

"I don't see why not."

"Because I'll be busy. I'll be working and going to school. I won't have time for a relationship. But even if I had time, I wouldn't pick M—" she caught herself almost saying Mac again, and quickly switched to "—Larry. We'd kill each other. In case you hadn't noticed, we fight like cats and dogs."

"That friend Shirley, I mentioned? She worked the kissing booth as well. And who should end up in her line? Stucky Peters. Those two had fought like cats and dogs as well, all through school. But Stucky, he kissed her and…well, it wasn't a quick peck on the lips. It was one of those long, special kisses. The other guys in line started hootin' and hollerin', but old Stucky he just held on to Shirley for dear life. That kiss—it was the beginnin' of the end for the two of them. Sometimes it's like that with kisses. A little peck on the cheek can change everything."

"What happened?" Mia asked.

"Well, they both tried to make a show of fighting, but it was as if the wind had gone outta their fightin' sails. Soon kissin' took priority, and after that…well, last I heard they had twelve grandchildren from their four kids."

"That's not going to happen with Ma…Larry and me." The problem she was having with Larry Mackenzie's name was that she was starting to think of him as Mac rather than Larry.

That just wouldn't do.

Names had power. And calling him Mac instead of Larry changed their relationship too much for Mia's comfort. She was going to force herself to think of him as Larry rather than Mac—a way of reminding herself that the only reason her relationship with Larry had changed was because of Katie.

When he found the baby a new home, they'd go back to their previous non-kissing, sniping sort of relationship.

Which was just the way Mia wanted it.

"Our kisses were just aberrations," she told Pearly. "We were stranded with a baby in a snowstorm. Unless that happens again, I think we're pretty much kiss-free."

She wasn't going to mention to Pearly that she'd kissed Larry again last night, with very little snow, no storm and a sleeping baby who caused very little stress.

"Now—" Pearly started, but the door to the office banged open and Mac came in with the car seat.

"Are you game again today?" he asked.

"No problem," she said, grinning as he held out the car seat.

The feeling of lightness that permeated her body was because she was going to get to spend time with Katie. It didn't have anything at all to do with seeing Mac...er, Larry.

Nothing at all.

"Hi, Pearly," Mac said.

"I came to see your baby," Pearly said, taking the car seat from him before Mia could.

"Not mine," he corrected quickly. Too quickly. "I've got to be in court again this morning, but I have a lunch meeting to start the adoption process rolling for her. We're going to find her the perfect family."

Mia wanted to say no. To find some excuse to keep Mac from starting the process. Katie didn't belong with strangers. The baby belonged with him.

Pearly unwrapped, unbuckled, unzipped and took off Katie's hat.

"Look at that hair. I haven't seen hair that red since I sat behind Mickey Martin. Aren't you a sweetie," she cooed as she lifted Katie from the car seat. "How on earth are you ever gonna give her away?"

"She was never mine, so there's no giving away. I'm just doing what her mother wanted…finding Katie a perfect home."

"And what if the perfect place for her is with you?" Mia couldn't help but ask.

He laughed.

It wasn't a jovial sound. Instead Mia heard something else in it again. Pain.

He'd been adamant from the outset that he wasn't keeping Katie. Now she asked herself, why?

She didn't think it was simply that he was a

young lawyer with a busy, growing practice. She'd sensed something more, something deeper in his denial this time.

"The perfect place for a child, any child, would never be with me," he assured her. Looking decidedly uncomfortable, he added, "I've got to go. You've everything under control?"

"Sure," Mia said. "No problem. Leland will be thrilled she's visiting again."

After he'd left, Pearly sat quietly holding the baby for a few minutes.

Quiet and Pearly…two words that rarely went together.

"She is beautiful," Pearly finally said. "It would be easy to lose your heart to her."

"Yes," Mia said. "It was."

"Sometimes love's like that. Easy. So easy you don't even realize it happened. And sometimes, love is a bit harder. It takes some work. I think that kind of love—the kind you have to work for, to fight for— I think that it's the stronger for it."

"Well, I love Katie and it feels awfully strong, no fighting or working involved."

"I'm sure you do," was all Pearly said as she handed the baby to her. "Well, I better get going. Thanks for introducing me. You just think on what I said."

"Sure, Pearly, I will," Mia promised as she bounced a delighted Katie on her knee.

She kissed the baby's forehead.

Yes, Katie was easy to love. No fighting or working involved with it.

Easy love.

That's just the way Mia liked it.

Chapter Seven

They'd fallen into a routine Mac realized the following Friday afternoon on his way back to the office.

Even though Brigitta's house was once again illness-free, Katie kept coming to the office to spend her days with Mia.

Actually, Mia claimed she was more of a scheduling director for the baby, than anything else. Katie had become the belle of the law firm, visiting the various attorneys throughout the day. A sort of unofficial mascot.

Leland Wagner was the worst offender.

"He snatches her all the time," Mia had complained, with a smile rather than any real ire.

Mia not only kept Katie every day, she came home with them as well. In just one short week, the routine felt…routine. A part of the new rhythm to Mac's life.

A part he found he was enjoying.

He counted on sharing a meal with Mia. He looked forward to trading stories about their days. They cared for Katie together, marveling in her every small development.

Mac was beginning to count on all of it, to look forward to their new partnership, their evenings together.

The only part he didn't like was Mia leaving each night.

Even with Katie in the house, when Mia left it seemed to lose some of its spark, some of its warmth.

And every night she left, he realized he hadn't managed to kiss her again.

And even worse, he realized he wanted to.

Every night when she said, "I'll see you and Katie in the morning," he wanted to pull her into his arms and kiss her senseless.

Kiss her and more.

But every night he let her go without so much as a chaste peck on the cheek. Knowing it was the right thing to do, that toying with a forever sort of woman wasn't just unwise, but cruel. But knowing it didn't stop him from longing to do so many things with her.

He tried to convince himself that this sudden attraction to Mia was simply gratitude for all the help she'd given him. But he suspected it might be something more.

And he was man enough to admit—if only to himself—that that suspicion scared him to the core.

He'd always dated women who understood the rules. Women who would come close, but only so close. When a relationship was done, there were no regrets, just some fond memories.

But that wasn't Mia. She wasn't casual. She was a happily-ever-after sort of woman. Which is why these feelings—his need to be with her—didn't make sense.

He realized he'd been musing about Mia and his out-of-whack feelings for her all the way from the courthouse to the office.

"Hey," she said with a smile as he walked in the door.

He purposely didn't stomp the snow off his feet, just to annoy her. But she was so busy telling him about Katie that she didn't even notice, which meant she wasn't annoyed, and wasn't sniping.

"…she spent most of the day playing with *Grandpa* Leland. If he's not with her, someone else is trying to get her. I almost need a sign-out sheet to keep track."

Mac smiled as he listened, but his eyes were focused on the brochure on Mia's desk. A college brochure.

"What's that?" he asked.

She looked down. "Oh. I'm thinking about finishing my degree."

"You'll be quitting here, then?" he asked, surprised at how gruff his voice sounded.

Mia didn't seem to notice. She just smiled and said, "No. You're not getting rid of me that easy, Larry. I'll need a job when I go back because I'll still need to eat."

Something eased in Mac's chest. Something he hadn't even realized had been clenched while he waited for her answer.

"I'm taking Katie with me this afternoon," was all he said, because if he said he was relieved she wouldn't be leaving she might take the comment for something other than it was. After all, who would he spar with if it wasn't for Mia?

She looked confused. "What's up?"

"Her mother's funeral." His answer sounded short even to his own ears.

Mia's expression softened to one of sympathy. He could hear it in her voice as well as when she said, "I'm sorry. I didn't know it was today."

"I didn't either until yesterday. I talked to the social worker. She said she hadn't been able to track down any family at all. Not surprising, really. That's why Marion O'Keefe came to see me. She had no one else."

"So who made the arrangements?" Mia asked. "The state?"

"Me."

Mac couldn't stand the thought of Marion O'Keefe all alone and unclaimed. Buried by the Commonwealth of Pennsylvania. Not mourned by anyone.

He might not have known her, but what he knew of her he admired. He'd not only watch over her daughter, but do this one last thing for Marion O'Keefe.

"You?" Mia asked.

"She's Katie's mother. She was a good mother. Concerned for her baby's future before she was even born. She deserves a real service. Kim Lindsay's sending over what few possessions Marion had."

"Where's the funeral?"

Mac shook his head. "It's just a graveside service. I don't know if Marion O'Keefe was religious or not, so, I thought something simple was best."

Mia nodded. "When and where?"

"Erie Cemetery at noon."

"Good. That's my lunch hour. I'll be there."

"You don't have to," he said.

"Neither did you. You didn't have to do any of this. Sign on as guardian for a stranger, step in and make final arrangements for a client. But you did, you are. So will I."

"Thanks," he said, taking Mia's hand and giving it a small squeeze.

She smiled at him. "You're a nice guy, Larry."

There was no heat in her voice as she said his

given name. Her smile warmed it, making it almost a pet-name rather than a way to needle him.

"Thanks, Mia. You're pretty nice yourself."

Realizing he was still holding her hand, he pulled his back. "Listen, can Katie stay with you a few more minutes while I run upstairs and return a few calls?"

"You know you don't even need to ask." She paused, then asked, "The calls? Are they about adoptive parents?"

"No. I met with people from the agency, but I don't know if I want to go through them. I'm still weighing my options."

He had the paperwork. All he had to do was sign it, and return it, and the ball would be set in motion.

The sooner he signed, the sooner Katie could find her family. The problem was, he wasn't sure the agency would get Katie the kind of family she deserved.

Oh, he could participate. He could interview, question prospective parents, but in the end, he could still pick the wrong people. People who might let Katie down.

Failing Katie wasn't an option.

Somehow he had to be sure that she'd get the kind of parents she deserved. The best.

"You're thinking about keeping her?" Mia asked, hope in her voice.

"No." He turned and went up the stairs without another word.

No. He might not know how to ensure Katie got the parents she deserved, but he knew she deserved more than he'd ever be able to give her.

Somehow he would figure it out.

Mia watched Mac storm up the stairs. Her question had obviously annoyed him.

Not that long ago, annoying Mac without even trying would have seemed like a bonus.

She looked at Katie who was dozing in her car seat. "He doesn't want to let you go, which is one of the big reasons he's going to let you go."

It didn't make sense to Mia.

But then not much about Mac had never made sense to Mia. The fact that she felt closer to him didn't change the fact she didn't understand him.

He was a puzzle. Every time she thought she had him figured, had found the right pieces and was going to finally put it all together, she realized she was even more confused.

This last week had shown her that Mac was worth figuring out, so she wasn't going to stop trying. But right now, she had other things to take care of.

She had calls to make.

Mac probably wouldn't be pleased. Asking for help or support wasn't something he did.

But Mia had no such compunctions.

She was going to ask, and when Mac got mad, she'd tell him she'd done it for Katie.

And in her heart of hearts she knew that for Katie, Mac would ask or do anything.

Mac held the well-bundled, squirming baby tight as he walked back to his car.

He turned and looked over his shoulder again.

He didn't know what to make of it.

It was freezing out. Another storm was threatening to blow in off the lake. The clouds were dark and ominous.

Not a fit day to be outdoors.

And yet, half the Square had given up their lunch breaks and turned out for Marion O'Keefe's service.

Almost the entire firm had come to the simple ceremony. Other people from the Square had come as well. Pearly, along with her sidekicks, Mabel and Josie. Libby, Josh, Louisa, Joe…

They'd all come to put Marion O'Keefe to rest. A woman they'd never met.

"You called them?" Mac said to Mia as they walked back to the car.

"Don't be mad," she said.

"I didn't need them. I—"

She interrupted him. "I know, the great Larry Mackenzie doesn't need or want anyone. But it

wasn't for you. It was for Katie. Someday you can
tell her that there were people here. That there were
flowers. Becca at the flower shop did a great job on
such short notice."

Mac had been struck by the flowers when he'd
first arrived. The arrangements looked incongruous
against the stark, snowy landscape.

"Katie deserves to know that people said goodbye
to her mother for her when she wasn't old enough to
do it herself," Mia said softly.

"Oh. I hadn't thought of that. They were here for
Katie."

He glanced again at the small group all walking
back to their cars.

They'd come for the baby. That he could understand.

"No," Mia said, shaking her head. "They're here
for you."

"Me?" He strapped Katie into her car seat, puzzling over that.

As he stood and shut the passenger door, Mia
lightly touched his cheek. "Mac, I don't think you realize how many friends you have."

The departing crowd suddenly made him nervous.
"I didn't ask."

"No. You didn't. You wouldn't. But I would and
did. For you. For Katie. For Marion O'Keefe. I think
Katie's mother was a special woman."

Some of his panic receded. For Marion and Katie. That's why the crowd had come out. That was easier to accept, than the thought that they had come for him.

That kind of friendship carried with it a burden that Mac didn't really want to accept. He didn't want to owe anyone because they might ask for repayment and he wouldn't be able to help them. He'd let them down.

Letting people down. It was in his genes. He might fight against it, try to avoid it, but still on a personal level, he didn't trust himself. He didn't want anyone to count on him.

"I didn't know Marion O'Keefe, other than those couple visits, but yes, I believe she was special."

Speaking of special women…Mac took Mia's hand and smiled at her, hoping she could tell how much he appreciated what she'd done.

She smiled back, giving his hand a small squeeze.

"Are you going back into the office?" she asked.

"I'm way behind in paperwork. I should use what's left of the afternoon to try and make a dent. But dinner after work?"

Every day he asked, and every day he held his breath until she answered.

"Sure," she said.

He exhaled and smiled.

"I'll cook tonight," she continued. "We've just about exhausted the local take-out options."

"We could stop and pick up tacos again. I know they're your favorite."

He even knew what her selections would be…nachos with everything and that chicken thing she always ordered.

"Even a favorite gets old if you do it too many times. I can handle cooking." She paused a moment, then asked, "You're not afraid to eat my cooking, are you?"

He walked around the car and got in. Mia was already buckling her seat belt.

"Can you cook?" he asked, rather than straight-out answer her question.

"I grew up with brothers…brothers who like to eat. Of course I can. I put all the ingredients in my car this morning."

She'd packed the ingredients. She'd been planning on coming home with him.

No. Not with him. For him. For Katie. All this was for Katie, he reminded himself.

But despite the warning he gave himself, he smiled.

"So what are we having?" he asked.

"My world-famous potato soup. That is, unless you don't like potato soup. If you hate it, we're back to take-out."

"Soup sounds perfect today," he admitted.

"After work then?" she asked.

"After work."

Perfect.

It wasn't just soup that sounded perfect…it was eating it with Mia Gallagher.

The thought disturbed him, but not enough to make him cancel.

Nothing could have made him cancel.

The great Larry Mackenzie doesn't need or want anyone.

The words had just slipped out, but Mia recognized the truthfulness in them. They'd nagged at her the rest of the day.

They were still nagging at her as she prepared dinner.

There was something in Mac that didn't want to let people in. He didn't hold them at arm's length. No, he invited them in with his humor and jokes, but only let them in so far.

Although they'd fallen into a comfortable relationship, a friendship with an occasional bout of their old banter to spice things up, truth was, Mac hadn't really let her in either.

He'd shared that one small story about his friend Chet and the makeshift sled. That was it.

She stirred the soup with a bit more gusto than necessary. It was something simple and filling. Perfect for a cold winter day.

"Come and get it," she called as she ladled up two

bowls. She set them on the table along with the crusty French bread and bowl of grated cheese.

"Wow," Mac said as he came into the kitchen cradling Katie. "At least it smells like you can cook."

Mia loved to see him hold Katie.

There was no distance, no staying safe. He might want to think there was, but the fact he'd fallen head-over-heels for Katie O'Keefe was evident.

"Want me to take her while you eat?" she asked.

"No. We've got a system. I will let you butter me a piece of bread though. I can eat one-handed, but haven't figured out buttering or cutting one-handed yet."

She laughed and obliged him. Setting a piece of buttered bread on his plate as he took his first sip of the soup.

He made a *mm*ing sound. "You didn't lie. You can cook."

"Like I said, two brothers with bottomless pits for stomachs helped me learn. I don't do fancy, but I do filling."

They ate in companionable silence for a few minutes. Katie gurgled happily to herself, content to sit on Mac's lap. Mia couldn't help but steal glances at the two of them. They were so right together.

Why didn't Mac see it?

"So, did you make any adoption headway?" she asked.

"I've started checking around, but haven't done much. I'm having a hard time thinking about placing her with strangers. The perfect solution would be to place her with someone I know, someone who would allow me to play benevolent uncle. Someone—"

He stopped mid-sentence and looked lost in thought.

"Mac?" Mia asked.

"I have an idea," he said, excitement in his voice.

"What?"

"No. Let me think about it some more before I say anything."

"But, Mac," she protested.

He finally focused back in on her and laughed. "You know, I've learned a lot about you recently. You're good with babies. You can cook. And I've learned that patience isn't one of your virtues."

"No. It's not," she said.

She knew she sounded petulant. She was petulant. She hated waiting. She was the kind of person who peeked at Christmas presents if she had a chance.

"I'll tell you soon. I just need to mull it over for a bit, to see if it could work."

Mia sighed. "Fine."

"Let's talk about that college brochure."

"You're changing the subject."

He laughed again. "Yes, I am."

Whatever new idea he'd had lightened his mood immensely.

"College? Tell me more," he prompted.

"What's to say? I'm seriously thinking about going back in the fall."

"Full-time?" he asked.

"Evenings and weekends. I talked to Mr. Wagner and he said if I need an afternoon or morning class, he'll work it out with me. Hanni and Liesl both already said they'd fill in."

"How many more credits do you need for your degree?"

"One year of credits, then student teaching, and I'll be official."

"A teacher?" he said slowly.

Mia geared up for one of his wisecracks, but all he said was, "You'd be good at it."

"I like kids. Someday I want my own. Three or four at least."

"Four?"

She laughed. "I know, big families are getting rarer, but I can't imagine life without my brothers. When I have kids, I want them to have siblings."

"But you've sacrificed so much for your brothers. You had to put everything on hold. If you'd been an only child, you'd have only had to worry about yourself."

"Being alone like that might mean less worries, but it's also lonely. Whatever I did for my brothers, it was worth it. Marty and Ryan deserved the chance."

"And you?" Mac pressed. "What did you deserve? Quitting school? Putting aside your own dreams?"

"I just put them on hold. And now, the boys have both graduated and it's my turn to fulfill those dreams. I'll get my degree, teach—"

"Find some man who will never really be worthy of you, marry him, have his kids and have given everything up all over again? That's your plan?"

"Mac, when you love someone and they love you, there's no *giving up* involved. You get back so much more than you *lose*. Watching Marty and Ryan succeed, knowing I helped make their dreams a reality, that's something worthwhile. They needed me after Mom died, and I was there."

He didn't look convinced.

Mia felt sorry for him. To live your life that alone, to never need anyone, never allow yourself to count on anyone. She knew she could never live like that.

"Since I cooked, you wash the dishes and I'll get Katie Cupcakes here ready for bed."

Mia might work at the firm while she was back in school, but she'd have to quit when she got her degree, Mac realized as he scrubbed the soup pot.

She'd leave and work at the job she'd always

dreamed of. He was happy for her. Happy that she was finally free to pursue her goals.

But he'd miss her at the office.

She brightened the place up, although he'd never say that to her.

She kept him on his toes, always willing to join him in a verbal sparring match. He'd miss that.

He'd miss her.

How on earth had that happened?

He dried the pan and put it back on its hook.

"She was out before I even laid her in the crib," Mia said, setting the baby monitor on the table. "But she'll probably be up again for a bottle before long."

"That's fine. I try to feed her right before I call it a night. Most of the time that's enough to keep her quiet until morning. And I kind of like that late feeding. It's dark and quiet. She has a habit of holding on to my shirt while she drinks the bottle, as if she's afraid I'll slip away."

Mac realized what he'd said. "Sorry. Sounding way too sappy for even me to stand."

"Not too sappy at all. It's nice to get an occasional glimpse of what goes on inside you."

She gave him a look.

It was a soft sort of look.

Mac had seen looks like that before, and they never boded well.

"Stop that," he said.

"What?"

"Looking at me like that."

"Like what?"

"Like you'd like to kiss me." And as troubling as Mia wanting to kiss him might be, the fact that he wanted to kiss her was even more so.

"Kick you?" she asked. "Mac, I can't help looking like I want to kick you. You're so darned kick-able."

She was deliberately misunderstanding him. He knew it. She knew it.

"Not kick, *kiss,*" he said. "You want to kiss me."

"No. I want to go home and relax."

"You can't relax here?"

"Relaxing around you is difficult, and occasionally impossible."

"Now, why do you suppose that is?"

"Because you're impossible?"

"No, I think the fact you can't relax around me leads me right back to my assumption that you want to kiss me."

"Mac—" she started to protest.

But Mac leaned over before she could get any further, and placed his lips on hers. She softened, leaning into him. Her arms wrapped around his neck and she deepened the kiss.

Tasting, probing, teasing until Mac thought he'd go insane with desire.

He scooped her up and carried her into the living room. He sat on the couch, pulling her onto his lap.

"We should stop," Mia whispered.

"Probably," he agreed. But rather than stopping, he kissed her again.

His hands slipped under her blouse, caressing the soft skin on her abdomen, slowly moving upwards. Needing to explore every inch of Mia Gallagher.

Needing—

"Waaaa…"

They both jumped at the sound. Mia jumped off Mac's lap. Mac jumped from the couch. "You'd better go get her, and I'd better get home," she said.

"Mia, we should talk—"

"Later. We'll talk later. Right now, I've got to go, and Katie needs you."

Damn, Mac thought as Mia bolted from the house. He hurried upstairs to the baby's room. She was sitting in her crib looking forlorn and alone.

Mac picked her up and cradled her.

He knew how she felt.

Every time Mia left he felt like Katie looked.

Lost and forlorn.

And he didn't like it.

Chapter Eight

A loud, incessant buzzing pulled Mia from one of the most erotic dreams she'd ever had. Mac had been running his hand lightly down...

There was another buzz. Longer.

Slowly she pried her eyes opened and looked at the clock.

Ten?

Ten o'clock on a Saturday morning and someone was at her door?

Mia groaned and put a pillow over her head. She'd hardly slept a wink last night. She'd tossed and turned, and when she did manage to fall asleep, she dreamed of Mac.

Kissing Mac.

And more.

Hands touching, exploring.

His hands.

Her hands.

And then…

If the kissing part was disturbing, the *and-more* and the *and-then* parts were even more so.

Disturbing.

Like the doorbell that was ringing again.

It nagged at her.

She couldn't ignore the fact she'd kissed Mac.

Just like she couldn't ignore the stupid bell.

Sighing, she got up and tossed on a robe, then shuffled to the front door of her small, first floor flat. She peeked out the door and groaned as she fumbled with the chain and the lock.

She opened the door and glared.

"Surprise," Mac said.

He had Katie's seat in one hand, and a white paper bag in the other as he walked into the apartment.

"So, are you ready?" he asked in a perky manner.

Perky wasn't a word she'd ever used to describe Mac, but it only made sense he'd be perky if he thought it might annoy her.

And first thing on a Saturday morning perky was more than annoying. The only thing saving Mac was that he'd carried in the car seat and the mysterious white bag…a bag that looked as if it could contain something worth waking up for.

"Earth calling Mia…are you ready?" he repeated.

"Ready to go back to bed," she grumbled, still eyeing the bag and trying to decide just what he brought.

"Ready to go out with Katie and me. We have a surprise for you. And it's practically balmy today, at least balmy if you consider it's winter in Erie. Mid-forties. The kind of day that makes you want to get outside and enjoy."

"It's the kind of day that makes me want to go back to bed." With whatever was in that bag. It was something good and gooey, she'd bet.

"Mornings aren't your best time of day, are they?" Mr. Chipper asked.

"No." The bag swung in a merry little way from Mac's hand. Taunting her.

Maybe bagels?

If he brought cream cheese and cinnamon spread she'd forgive him for waking her.

"Would it help if I said I brought donuts?"

Ah, donuts.

Mia felt a bit perkier herself. "It would depend on what kind."

"Chocolate cream-filled from Mighty Fine."

"Okay, that might tempt me into waking up early on my day off."

"And we all know tempting you is what I do best," he said, placing the bag on the table as he began to unbundle the baby.

"Annoying me, that's what you do best," Mia said as she opened the bag.

"Ambrosia," she murmured as the sweet smell tickled her nose. She helped herself to a donut.

"The fact that I annoy you so easily makes the fact that I tempt you sort of a conundrum of sorts, doesn't it?" he asked as he lifted Katie from her seat.

"Larry," was all Mia said in response.

She couldn't say more because she took a huge bite of the donut and groaned with the pleasure of the sweet chocolate taste.

She chuckled when she saw him wince.

"I thought you'd given up the Larrys and decided to call me Mac like the rest of the world," he groused.

"I would never give up part of my arsenal. I just use Larry with a bit more discretion now."

She took the rest of the donut and padded into the small efficiency kitchen to start the coffee while Mac bounced Katie on his knee.

The baby gurgled her happiness as Mia took another bite.

"Mmm" was her appreciative comment. "You might be annoying, but you do manage good surprises."

"That's not the surprise. That's just breakfast."

Mac looked altogether too pleased with himself.

"So where's the surprise?" she asked, feeling cautious.

"Go get dressed and I'll show you."

"I don't know, Larry," she said. "You've got a certain gleam in your eye. It's making me nervous."

There was a lot about Mac that made her nervous. The fact that she'd like nothing more than to walk over and plant a big kiss on his cheek…that made her more nervous than the look in his eye.

"Go get your shower and you won't be able to see my gleam."

"Fine." She took the last bite of her donut and headed back to the bathroom wondering just what Larry Mackenzie was up to.

And despite her best intentions, she hoped it might include a kiss or two. Maybe even some and-more and and-then.

"So just where are we going?" Mia asked for the umpteenth time as they cruised up Peach Street.

"Don't you trust me?" Mac asked, doing his best to look innocent.

"Once again, about as far as I can throw you, Larry," she said.

He was pleased to note there was no spite in her voice, just a gentle teasing.

"Well, you don't have to throw me anywhere. We're almost there."

It was still a bit too early for much traffic, even on Peach Street, which was affectionately—and frequently non-affectionately—known as Peach Jam.

Even if it had been wall-to-wall traffic, Mac would still be grinning. He felt like a kid at Christmas, sort of heady with anticipation.

"Close your eyes," he instructed.

"Come on, Larry." Exasperation tinged her voice.

"Close them."

He glanced over and saw that she had complied.

Would wonders never cease?

Mia Gallagher had just listened to him.

"Just another minute," he said as he pulled into the car lot, stopped the Explorer and put it into Park. "Keep them closed."

"Mac," she complained.

He was grinning as he got out of the car, walked around it and opened her door. "Come on."

"What about the baby."

"We're not going anywhere. She's fine."

"But—"

"Open your eyes."

Mia did, scanned the lot, then looked back at him, a question in her eyes.

"You said you were looking for a new car. How about this? Jeep Cherokee. Four-wheel drive. Leather seats. Seat-warmer. Automatic ignition. Two years old, so it's not brand-new, but it's new used. And my buddy says the owner trades in his car every two years like clockwork. They're mint."

"But…"

"I'm not saying you have to buy it. I'm just saying it sounded like what you were looking for, so I thought I'd bring you up to look at it before Frank puts it on the market."

"If it's not on the market yet, how did you find out about it?"

"After you mentioned you were looking for something new, and what you wanted, I gave him a call and told him to keep an eye out."

She stood there staring at the Cherokee. "I don't know."

"Why don't you try it." He reached in his pocket. "Frank gave me the keys."

"You went to a lot of trouble setting this up," she said slowly, giving him an odd look.

"Not that much trouble," Mac said, suddenly feeling uncomfortable. "I do some work for Frank and just mentioned it in passing."

"Still. It was nice." She shook her head. "Mac, you're—" She stopped short. "I don't suppose taking it for a little ride could hurt."

Mac wished she'd finished her sentence. He was… *what?* He wanted to ask, but didn't. Instead he said, "Great. Let me just move Katie's car seat over. Here, press this button. The car will start and warm up."

Mia did as directed and the car roared to life.

"And this one…it will heat the front seats."

She pushed the other button.

She stood there staring at the car as Mac moved the baby's seat into the back, and strapped it in.

"Mia," he said. "Are you going to get in, or are you going to just stand there."

"Getting in."

She climbed into the driver's seat and Mac got in on the passenger side.

He heard her give a little sigh of contentment as she settled into the well-warmed seat.

She turned to him and smiled.

That smile twisted something in his gut. It made him want to reach across the seat and pull her into his arms.

Watching her this morning in her ratty robe, with her bed-head hair, eating a donut made him want to kiss her.

Having her snipe at him, or laugh with him made him want to kiss her…and more.

The want was quickly turning to something stronger, something more like need.

He realized he'd taken her hand. It was happening more and more often, him reaching out and touching her without even thinking about it.

Quickly, he pulled his hand back and said, "Are you ready?"

"Where should we go?" she asked.

"Wherever you want. Frank won't be in for about an hour. We've got it until then to decide if you like it."

"Why?" she asked, looking confused.

"Why? Because if you don't want it, Frank will try and sell it today. If you do want it, we'll start the paperwork."

"No." She shook her head. "What I meant was, why did you go to all this trouble?"

Mac didn't like the way she was looking at him. It was a sort of soft and warm look. He didn't want her getting soft and warm feelings about him.

He didn't want to exchange casual touches with her.

He didn't want to dream about her. To want to call her all the time.

He didn't want to need to be with her, to see her smile, to hear her laugh.

He didn't want to want her, but here he was wanting and doing regardless.

He could try warning her off, but last time he'd tried that she'd broken into laughter. And the trouble with warning her off was there was no one warning him off.

He simply said, "It wasn't any trouble. I was talking to Frank and mentioned that I had a friend looking for a car. I told him what you wanted and he called back last night with this."

"But why do you care?" she asked, pushing.

"I don't know. But don't read too much into it," he warned.

He waited half a beat for her to laugh, but she didn't. She still sat in the driver's seat, staring at him.

"Maybe I'd just like to see Frank make a nice commission off you?" There. That sounded good and snipey.

"I don't think so," she said softly.

"Fine. So, maybe the fact you were driving that jalopy was making me a nervous wreck. Erie's not a place for bald tires in the winter. I'd feel better knowing you had reliable transportation."

"But—"

"Why do you care why I did it? The baby's in the back not crying and you're sitting in a car with all the gizmos you wanted. So why don't you stop questioning me and just drive?"

Mia shot him one more, odd, assessing look, then pulled out of the car lot.

Mac reached over and clicked on the radio.

"Just checking out the sound system," he said.

In reality he needed some buffer to keep Mia from asking any more questions…questions he couldn't answer.

"So, what did you think?" Mac's friend Frank asked.

What did she think?

Mia glanced at Mac, holding Katie.

She thought it was actually very easy to learn to like Mac. But that had changed. Something more than liking was going on.

Something deeper.

Stronger.

Something like…love.

The word kept creeping into her thoughts.

Love?

Loving Mac?

She sighed, admitting the truth to herself.

She loved Mac.

It was a quiet feeling that had stolen into her heart somewhere in between the sniping and the liking.

Mia thought learning to love Mac wasn't all that hard. As a matter of fact, loving him was quite easy.

She remembered him warning her not to fall in love with him. She'd laughed, but maybe the last laugh was on her. Because although loving Mac was easier than she'd ever imagined, getting him to allow her to love him…now that could be hard.

Was she up to the challenge?

"Mia," Mac said. "What did you think?"

"I'll take it."

Take the car…and take a chance on loving a man who might never open up enough to love her back.

Chapter Nine

The following Friday morning Mac stood at Mia's desk, looking oddly uncomfortable.

But he couldn't be as uncomfortable as she felt.

It had been a long week.

Katie had spent her days with Brigitta. Mia had driven to work each day in her new car. She'd gone back to Mac's each night, helped with the baby, and shared a meal.

What she wanted to do was share her newfound feelings.

But she didn't.

Just like at this moment she wanted nothing more than to reach up and stroke his cheek, to comfort him, but she wouldn't.

Instead she said, "You wanted something?"

"Uh…"

"Yes," she said, when he paused and didn't continue.

"Listen, I'm heading down to Pittsburgh tomorrow morning."

"And you want me to keep Katie?" A whole day with Katie…without the ever-present tension she felt around Mac.

She'd like that.

She'd missed spending her days with the baby now that Katie was staying at Brigitta's. Oh, she'd still seen her every evening, but her new feelings for Mac made the evenings feel…awkward. It made it difficult to even enjoy Katie.

Yes, a whole day with just Katie and none of the strain she felt around Mac was great.

"No," he said, quashing her plans. "I'd like you to come along. You could drive and test out the new ride on the highway."

"Why Pittsburgh?"

"It's just dinner at the Zumigalas'. It's no big deal if you have other plans."

But it was a big deal.

Mia could see that.

The invitation had nothing to do with test-driving her car.

Mac was taking her to meet the Zumigalas. There was something different about them, about the way his voice softened when he mentioned them, or Chet. There was a vulnerability there.

A connection.

Larry Mackenzie might seem like the life of the party, but she'd come to realize he didn't have a lot of connections. He always kept himself a hand-span away. Giving himself distance.

But not with the Zumigalas.

And now he wanted her to meet them.

The thought warmed Mia and she felt a sudden surge of hope. Maybe if she met the Zumigalas she could discover how they'd reached Mac…maybe she could learn to reach him, as well.

"I'd love to come and meet them, if you're sure it's all right. It would be fun to test-drive the new car."

"And knowing that Katie's not the best traveler, I thought it might be wise to bring along reinforcements."

Some of Mia's pleasure faded.

He wasn't taking her because of some need to let her in, to open the door to his past just a bit. She was a convenience.

Still, she kept her smile in place. "What time?"

"Is eight too early? It's about a two-and-a-half-hour ride."

"No, that's perfect."

The next morning Mia waited nervously for Mac and Katie. She was meeting people Mac cared for in a way she was afraid he'd never care for her. Maybe she could learn something from them, figure out how to get beyond Mac's walls.

Or maybe she'd discover that her feelings for him were simply that they were spending so much time together. As soon as he found Katie a home they'd see less of each other and the sparks would die out.

She'd realize what she felt wasn't love. That this all-encompassing feeling was just an illusion.

Even as she thought the words, she realized she didn't believe them.

Her feelings for Mac just kept growing. It wasn't anything big he did. It was the little things. Buying her a coat, finding her a car…the way he treated Katie, all the pro bono work he did.

It might be easier if this feeling was an illusion, but every time she saw him, it grew bigger, heavier, more real.

Mac pulled up in front of her building and Mia had her coat on before he got out of his Explorer.

She put aside thoughts of her feelings, and hurried out.

"You're fast. Most women make a guy wait," as he unclipped the car seat from his car.

"I'm not most women," she said with a laugh.

Rather than coming up with some Larry-ish quip, he simply shot her an odd look and said, "No, I guess you're not."

He transferred Katie into her Cherokee and got in the passenger side.

Katie was asleep before they hit I 79.

Mac was quiet.

Mia watched the countryside fly by and finally, just outside Meadville, she said, "So, tell me about the Zumigalas."

She wasn't quite sure Mac would comply.

Other than telling her of the sledding incident, and mentioning he lived with them while he was in high school, he hadn't said much about them.

No surprise there…Mac didn't say much about anything personal. Mia should respect his privacy, but instead she wanted to dig in and find out more about him.

When he didn't say anything, she prompted, "You lived with them while you went to high school? They're your friend Chet's parents?"

"Yes."

"So what are they like?" She glanced at Mac, he wore an odd, faraway expression.

"Mr. Z. is quiet," he finally admitted. "He doesn't say much. I guess that's why when he does say something, everyone listens."

"And Mrs. Zumigala?"

"She's not quiet."

She glanced his way again, and he was grinning.

"Actually, you remind me of her in some ways," he added.

"You're saying I'm not quiet either? Is that a polite way of saying I have a big mouth?"

"Me, polite?" He chuckled. "No. What I meant was, until you, Mrs. Z. was one of the only people who wasn't afraid to call me on things."

"And did you need calling often?" she asked.

He laughed. "You don't know the half of it." And then he launched into some stories of his youth.

Mac got quiet again. Oh, he gave her directions, but had obviously shared all he was going to.

Mia eased the car into the driveway of a neat, white, split-level house. It had a two-car garage with a basketball hoop situated above and between the two forest-green doors. The yard was framed by a wooden fence and a few bushes were scattered throughout the yard.

The Zumigalas' house looked like a home.

Mia wondered if Mac and his friend Chet had played pickup games there.

She glanced over at him.

Yeah, she bet they did.

There was a winter-bare tree to the left of the drive. Not huge, but enough to provide a bit of shade in the summer. She could almost picture Mac sitting under it.

"It's good to be ho—" Mac started, then switched to "here."

Home.

He hadn't said home.

There was significance in the omission.

They got out of the car and Mac got Katie out of the back as Mia pondered the what's and why's of his word choice.

She didn't get to ponder long. The front door of the house opened and a dark-haired woman rushed out and toward the car.

"Mac," she said, her face alight with a smile.

"You don't have a coat on," Mac grumbled as she pulled him into a hug.

"Mac has a thing about coats," Mia said with a laugh.

The woman turned to her, and gave her a quick once-over. "You must be Mia."

"Guilty as charged, but I'm probably not guilty of anything else Mac told you about me. He exaggerates."

"He says he couldn't have gotten along without you."

"See, exaggeration. Mac doesn't need anyone in order to get along."

"Much as I'm enjoying the conversation," Mac said, "maybe we should get the baby inside?"

"Oh, my, where are my manners, come in, come in."

She hustled them into the house and shut the door. "Here, give me your coats." She hung them in the closet and shouted, "Sal, they're here."

Sal Zumigala was shorter than Mac. Shorter and

rounder. But he had a quiet smile when he spied them. "Good to see you, son."

"Nice to see you, Mr. Z."

"Let's go in and sit down," his wife said. "As much as I'm glad to see you, Mac, I want to see the baby."

She oohed and aahed as Mac unpacked Katie with the efficiency of an expert.

"She's beautiful." She held out her arms. "Let me have her."

Mac handed her over and smiled. "I knew you'd want to get your hands on her."

"I love babies," Mrs. Z. murmured as she started cooing to Katie, who cooed right back.

"And she likes you."

As Mac's Mrs. Z. held Katie Mia noticed the ring she was wearing.

"That's a beautiful ring," she said.

Mrs. Zumigala smiled. "Sal gave it to me on our last anniversary. It's a Celtic Knot."

She shot her husband a look that was so full of love it was palpable.

Mia sat back and watched the Zumigalas and Mac chat about this and that.

It wasn't so much what any of them said, but Mia could feel the love they shared. Mac was more open with them than she'd ever witnessed. No jokes to keep them away, just open, honest emotions.

They were as tangled together as the gold knot on Mrs. Zumigala's finger.

They were a family.

Mrs. Zumigala reluctantly handed the baby back to Mia as she served dinner.

Mia was getting to be an expert at juggling the baby on one knee while eating. Keeping Katie back far enough so she couldn't reach the plate.

"You look very natural holding her," Mrs. Z. said. "I remember when Chet was little. He liked to help me eat."

"Katie does, too," Mia said with a laugh. "I learned the hard way after I got a lap full of tacos one night at dinner. I'd prefer keeping the roast on my plate. It's delicious."

"Thank you. I like to cook. I miss having the boys home for dinners every night. It's different cooking for just Sal and me."

"Maybe you should have more kids," Mac said.

Mrs. Zumigala laughed. "I don't think that's in the cards, dear.

"Let me just clear the table, and then I'll see about our dessert. Double chocolate cake. It's Mac's favorite."

"Before dessert, I'd like to talk to you both," Mac said. "Mia, would you mind if I talk to Mr. and Mrs. Z. alone for a minute?" he asked.

Mia picked up the baby and said, "Sure. Katie-

Cupcakes and I will go turn on the game in the living room."

She shot Mac a smile as she left the room.

Mac smiled back. He probably shouldn't have invited Mia along, but he needed her here. He needed her smile, needed to have her near.

"What's wrong, son?" Mr. Zumigala asked when Mia had left.

"I—" Mac stopped short, not sure how to say what he'd come here to say.

He'd gone over it again and again in his mind, lining up arguments just like he might for a court case. But unlike court, now that the moment was here and the Zumigalas were waiting for him to say something, he couldn't find the words.

"It's about Katie," he finally managed.

"Oh, honey," Mrs. Z. bubbled happily, "she's such a doll. And we can see that you've fallen in love with her. We're so happy for you. I've said for years that you need a family, haven't I, Sal?"

Mr. Z. nodded.

"Me?" Mac asked, incredulously. "You think I'm going to tell you that I'm keeping Katie?"

"You're not?" Mrs. Z's smile faded. "I don't see how you can let her go. I watched how you were with her, with Mia as well. The three of you mesh. You fit. You're a family."

"No," Mac said with more force than he'd intended. Being a family wasn't in the cards for him. He knew that.

He would have thought Mrs. Z. would recognize that fact.

"No," he said softer this time. "Mia's a friend. If you'd asked me a couple of weeks ago how I'd describe her, that wouldn't be the word I use, but there it is. She's a good friend. And Katie, well, you're right, I've lost my heart to her, but because I care I want the best for her, and that will never be me. I'm not a good candidate for parenting."

The Zumigalas sat quietly waiting for the rest of what he was going to say.

They were good at that.

Waiting.

They'd waited when he'd first moved in, waited for him to accept that they cared, that he was staying. Waited for him to realize his potential, trusting he'd follow their advice and try.

Now, they waited to hear what he had to say, trusting in it, in him.

"That's what I wanted to talk to the two of you about. Katie," he said.

Again, he had a hard time finding the words. He wondered why. Finding words generally came easily to him.

"I want to talk to you about adopting her," he finally said in a rush. Before they could respond he hurriedly continued, "I want the best for her, and I could spend the next couple months looking and I'd never find anyone better to raise her. You two…"

He stopped. He had the words this time, but felt uncharacteristically choked up.

"You didn't have to take me in. You just did. And you never made me feel like a burden. You—"

"Stop right there before you say something that will make me want to smack you," Mrs. Z. said.

Smacking was one of her favorite threats when he and Chet were in school. But to the best of Mac's knowledge, Mrs. Z. wouldn't even smack a housefly. The threat had always made them smile, and despite his emotional turmoil, Mac smiled this time as well.

"Listen to me, young man," she said, shaking a finger at him. "Maybe I didn't make myself clear in the past, so I'm going to put this as succinctly as I can. You never were a burden. You were a joy. The minute I met you I knew you were special. And when your aunt went into the hospital and you came to stay with us, I knew I'd have a hard time letting you go back to her. It was a relief when she went to live with her friend in Florida and agreed that you could stay here with us. It was a relief because you were mine."

She thumped her hand over her heart. "Mine. I knew it. I might not have given birth to you, but you're mine every bit as much as Chet is. You might call me Mrs. Z., and maybe you don't even think of me as such, but I'm your mother. In my heart, you're my son. You have been since the day you came to stay with us."

She crossed her arms over her chest, as if daring him to disagree.

Mac didn't.

Couldn't.

He was speechless. She'd told him she loved him before. He'd never quite believed her. He'd always felt as if there were some unstated qualifier.

She loved him, but then she loved everyone. It was in her nature.

But this vehemence in her words, this wasn't a casual sort of love. This was something different. Something bigger than he'd ever suspected.

"Me and Sal, we wanted a big family, but it never worked out. I used to wonder why, why we weren't blessed with more children. But then you came along and I found out I did have another son. I realized that family wasn't something you gave birth to, it's something you create. You're family."

He felt as if something new was lodged in his throat. He wasn't quite sure how to shake it. So he ignored and pushed around it, asking, "Maybe Katie's like that, too? Family you never knew you had?"

"Of course she is," Mrs. Z. said. "I knew the minute I saw her that she was my family, every bit as much as you are. The heart knows family when it sees it."

He felt a wave of relief. "So, you'll take her."

"No," she said.

"No?" Mac asked. "But, you said—"

"She's family. I love her, but I can't adopt her. I'm not as spry as I used to be, and you need to be quick on your feet to keep up with a little one. With that red hair and gleam in her eye, she's going to be busy and fast. I wouldn't be able to keep up."

"I don't understand."

His heart sank. He'd been so sure he'd found a solution, that the Zumigalas would fall in love with Katie and keep her. After all, they'd kept him. Katie was so much more loveable than he was.

"I won't adopt her," Mrs. Z. repeated, "but I've wanted grandchildren for years, right Sal?"

Mr. Z. nodded.

"And I've got my first one right out there in the living room. I'll spoil her rotten. You'll try to stop me, like any good father would, but I won't listen."

"I can't be her father," Mac said.

He'd said it to Mia, and now he'd said it to the Zumigalas.

He'd said it to himself countless times.

He couldn't be Katie O'Keefe's father.

Not hers.

Not anyone's.

"Why, I'd like to know?" Mrs. Z. asked.

"Look at my parents, my family. We're not the type to stick around. My mom and dad left me, my aunt couldn't wait to hand you responsibility for me. It's in the genes."

"You couldn't be more unlike those people who gave birth to you," Mrs. Z. said. "I thought you were smart enough to figure that out. Those people that you were born to were takers. And though you know I don't like speaking badly of anyone, they weren't very smart ones at that. They took your love, then threw it aside. You, you're a giver. You've got one of the biggest hearts I've ever met."

"Listen, boy," Mr. Z. said, "I've watched you carry this burden around for years. I figured you were smart and would eventually figure it out, but seems I was wrong. So, let me spell it out. You're nothing like the people who gave birth to you."

Mrs. Z. nodded. "Remember that first term in high school when you brought me your report card?"

Mac wouldn't ever forget that day. "You looked at it, and then at me. I could see you were disappointed. You asked if it was the best I could do."

"And you said no," she said. "I told you that grades were important because they gave you options. You could slide through high school, just getting by. But you'd be losing opportunities. What if you decided you wanted to be a brain surgeon? You'd never make it into school. Good grades left all the doors open to you, left all your options open. I wanted you to have them all. You listened and brought home A's from then on. You got that scholarship to college, then went on to law school. I was so proud of you."

Something warm spread through Mac's chest at her words. He'd made her proud.

"But," she continued, "for years you've been slamming doors on your personal options, just like you're doing now with Katie. You haven't even considered that maybe she wasn't given to you to find a home for, maybe she's part of the family that you could have if you're not too afraid to open the door."

"Mac," Mr. Z. said. "You're my son. I couldn't love you more, be more proud of you, if you'd been born to us. I don't think you're the type of man to let fear stand in the way of a gift. A true and utter gift. That's what that baby is."

"Mia, too, I think," Mrs. Z. said.

"I don't—" Mac started.

"Don't make any decisions now. Think on it, son. You have options…if you're not too afraid to take the wonderful chances that are sometimes handed to you."

Mrs. Z. hugged him. Hugged him hard. "But no matter what you do, what you decide, you're mine. Don't you forget that. I love you."

"I love you, too…" He paused, wanting to say

more. The word, that one word was lodged in his throat, aching to come out.

"Mom," he finally whispered. Louder, he said, "I love you, too, Mom."

Mrs. Z. started to cry. Hard earnest sobs.

"I'm sorry, I shouldn't have—"

With tears running down her face she still managed to give him a look, one of those looks.

"Don't you dare apologize. I've been waiting years to hear you call me that."

"What?"

"You know, for a smart boy, sometimes you're very slow." She pulled a tissue from her pocket and wiped her eyes. "But that just shows how much you mean to me, because despite your occasional denseness, I love you like crazy."

Mr. Z. slapped his back. "Me, too."

"Thanks…Dad."

Mr. Z. beamed.

"But about Katie—"

"No. Not another word about it. No decisions either. Give yourself time. Weigh your options. You know what you're doing. I'm sure you'll figure it out. Give yourself the time to make the right decision."

"But—"

"Now, let's go check on Mia and Katie before they think we've deserted them." She kissed his cheek. "We still have a chocolate cake that needs eating."

* * *

Mac knew that Mia was wondering what he'd discussed with the Zumigalas, but she didn't ask. They road in silence back to Erie. Katie slept almost the entire way.

Because Mia was driving, he simply stared out the window, thinking about what Mrs. Z., Mom, had said.

Keep Katie?

He wasn't sure he could do it. Part of him wanted to, knew that letting her go would be torture.

He loved her. He didn't doubt that. But he just didn't think he was the best choice for a parent.

And Mia?

He kept glancing at her as she drove.

She had finished putting her brothers through school. She had plans. This car was just the first step. She wanted to go back to school, finish her degree. She wouldn't have time for a relationship. Not that he wanted a relationship with her.

He realized suddenly they were home.

She turned off the ignition and looked at him, her blue eyes looking so seriously at him.

"Mac, I have something I want to say. Something you probably aren't going to want to hear."

"This seems to be the day for people telling me things they're not sure I want to hear. So go ahead."

"That day when you told me about your parents, you said you never wanted kids because you were afraid you'd be like them. I didn't ask for details, and after today, I don't need to. You see, I just met your parents…your real parents. I'm sorry, I couldn't help but overhear your conversation. You know, families aren't made by blood, but by love. The Zumigalas are your family. If you give Katie half the love they gave you, she'll be lucky."

Mia leaned across the seat, kissed his cheek and hurried out of the car before Mac could reply.

She went straight into her apartment, leaving him to put the baby back in his car.

He was on the road heading home, mulling over Mrs. Z. and Mia's words.

Family.

Mac had never really given any thoughts to a definition for that word before.

He'd always just assumed that it was genetics. Your family was the luck of the draw. And he'd drawn the short stick.

But then he'd found Mr. and Mrs. Z. She was right. She'd always treated him like a son. Just like Chet had always treated him as more of a brother than a friend.

Mac had been the one to hold back. To keep his distance. Not that they seemed to notice. The Zumigalas simply kept pushing, kept breaking down barriers.

Mac realized that Mrs. Z. had broken down his last one today. She was right, she was his mother in all the ways that mattered.

And Mia was right, if he could be half the parent that the Zumigalas were, then Katie would be all right.

And, with sudden clarity, he realized something else. He wanted to…he wanted to keep Katie, wanted to have a chance to watch her grow up.

He might not be the best choice, but he knew that he'd never find anyone who could love the baby as much as he did.

The reason he hadn't been looking very hard to find parents for her was that he hadn't wanted to trust someone else to do what he wanted to do.

Wanted almost more than anything else he'd ever wanted.

But Katie deserved more than just a father.

She deserved a whole family. She deserved…

Mia.

He'd known for a while now that he wanted Mia. He was drawn to her. He'd tried to convince himself that it was just a sexual pull, but it wasn't.

He wanted her to be part of his family because— the words that came so hard earlier came much easier now—because he loved her. He didn't want her just as Katie's mother. He wanted her.

Mia Gallagher.

He wanted her to help him raise Katie. Wanted to have other children with her. Babies with her smile, with her laugh.

He wanted to grow old with her.

Not just want.

He needed her.

He loved her.

But Mia had plans. She'd finally raised her brothers. Was finally going back to school and following her dream. Could he take that from her?

Would asking her to be his wife, to be Katie's mom be fair? She'd worked so hard and waited so long for her chance at happiness.

Mac didn't know.

"I don't know what to do," he admitted aloud to the sleeping baby.

Mac had always known what he wanted, where he was going. But now, he didn't have a clue.

"I do know one thing. I'm done looking for an adoptive family. You're mine. I know I'll screw up, but I swear, I'll always love you and try."

That was the best he could do for Katie.

The question remained, what was the best thing he could do for Mia?

Chapter Ten

Mia spent her weekend thinking about what she'd said to Mac. He would be a fantastic father, but she doubted he'd listen to her. He was stubborn like that.

He'd warned her not to fall in love with him, warned her that he was giving Katie away.

Well, she couldn't make him love her, but he couldn't stop her from loving him.

And she couldn't stop him from giving up Katie, but if he wouldn't raise the baby, there was another option. One that just sort of snuck into her mind. One she couldn't seem to shake.

If Mac wouldn't raise Katie…Mia would.

It was so simple she couldn't believe it had taken her so long to figure it out.

She'd adopt Katie.

She'd raise her and love her.

Mac could still be a part of the baby's life. Part of Mia's life.

He was stubborn. He'd probably argue against the idea, saying he didn't want Katie raised by a single mother. But Mia would line up her arguments.

If he was too stubborn, she'd call in Mrs. Zumigala. She bet Mac's surrogate mother would pick up her cause.

Somehow she'd make Mac see she was meant to be Katie's mother. And someday, maybe they could get him to see he was meant to be her father…meant to be with Mia.

Decision made, Mia agonized over how to broach the subject.

She knew Mac was going to argue. He had very specific requirements for Katie's parents. She knew she fell short. But she also knew that no one would ever love the baby as intensely as she did.

That had to count for something…didn't it?

She arrived at his house Sunday afternoon, Teresa's subs in hand.

Her stomach was twisted with tension. Her roast beef sub was untouched. Katie bounced happily on her knee, unaware that her fate was about to be decided.

"Mac?" Mia asked.

He didn't respond. He was staring out the window again. He'd seemed distracted all afternoon.

"Mac?" she said again.

"Sorry. I was thinking."

"Is everything okay? You've been a bit out of it?"

"Fine," he said.

Mia didn't believe him. He might have a lawyer's ability to mask his feelings, but with Mac, she could see through it. He'd been quiet and pensive since they'd visited his parents.

"You're upset the Zumigalas wouldn't take Katie."

"I had hoped they would. They would have been a perfect solution."

"I know. I thought about it all last night. And I have an idea. I don't think you'll be very enthused about it, at least not at first. So I want you to hear me out before you react."

"What?" he asked, suddenly, totally, focused on her.

Mia was afraid she'd never get it all out before he nixed her idea, so she said, "Swear you'll just sit there and let me say this."

"Fine," Mac said.

Mia waited.

He sighed and raised his right hand. "I swear."

She smiled and took a deep breath before blurting out, "I found the perfect place for Katie."

"I thought you said being with me was the perfect place for Katie?"

"But you won't keep her. So I came up with a solution. Let me raise her."

She waited for the explosion, but Mac kept his promise and just sat there, staring at her, waiting for the rest.

"I know you've been looking at families, at a traditional mother and father arrangement for her, but I want you to consider letting me adopt her. I know it will be a struggle, but I've been there…done that. I might not have a lot of money, but I have a lot of love. I want her, Mac. I don't know how else to say it. It's not just want…it's a need. She's part of me. If you give her to someone else, I'll grieve because I know you'll never find her someone who can love her like I can. They may be able to provide a more financially stable home, but I can give her love. So much love."

"What would you do with her while you work?" he asked.

"Day care, I guess. I know it's not the perfect solution, but I can make it work. I called and talked to Brigitta this morning. She's willing to keep her. You know how much she loves kids. And my brothers, they'll love her. They'll be great uncles. She might not have a traditional father figure, but the boys would fill in."

"Mia, what about your dreams?" he said softly. "You have a car with a seat-warmer, and what about going back to school? Finally living life for yourself?

You've earned that. Putting your brothers through school, you've earned time for your own dreams."

"That's what I thought as well, but it turns out, Katie is my dream. I want to be her mother, Mac. As for college, I'll go back someday. It will be there. You're never too old to stop learning. My degree can be finished whenever I'm ready."

"If you keep putting off your own goals in order to serve everyone else, you may never be ready, there may never be a right time. You keep giving up your dreams to serve others. First your brothers, now Katie."

"Then so be it. I told you before, there's no real giving up involved when you love someone. I love my brothers, and I love Katie. Going to college isn't going to make me happier. Maybe more employable, but not happier. Katie will make me happier."

She wanted to add, *the only thing that could make me happier than having Katie in my life, would be having you there, too.* But Mac had made his feelings on a relationship clear. He'd shut the door on it as firmly as he'd shut the door on the idea of keeping Katie himself.

Mia wished she could open the door for him. Maybe if she kept trying, eventually she'd get it to crack open. If not, she'd just keep breaking her heart, ramming against the door to his. It was a chance she was willing to take.

"Please," she said. "Having Katie is one of my biggest dreams."

"One? You have more?" he asked.

She wanted to say, *just one…you.* Instead, she said, "Well, there's school. I'll do it, too. I know I will."

"That's it?"

"Dreams are private things, Mac. There's one more, but it's a fool's dream. I've seen that. So, I've put it aside. But being Katie's mom, that's something I can do."

He shook his head and Mia's heart sank. He wasn't going to let her raise Katie.

"I wish I could say yes, Mia," he said softly, "but I can't. You see, I already found a family for her. I've promised."

"Oh." She could feel the tears gather around her eyes.

"Don't," he said, his voice raw with emotion as he brushed away a tear. "Don't."

"I'm sorry." She swiped at her eyes. "I know you're doing what you feel is best, that you want Katie to have a traditional, stable family."

And she knew why he wanted that so desperately for Katie. He'd never had that. He'd been abandoned as a child. He wanted to be sure Katie never had to deal with that.

Understanding didn't stop her heart from breaking, but for Mac's sake, she'd put her misery away until later.

"Tell me about Katie's perfect family," she said softly.

"They're not perfect, but it's their imperfections that make them perfect for Katie," Mac said. "You see, I've learned a lot these last few weeks. The only real definition for family is a group of people held together by love. I have that with the Zumigalas. I wasn't born into my true family, I found them. And I've found Katie's family as well. Her new father's got a bit of emotional baggage, but he's dealing with it. Her new mother…well, she's darn near perfect. She's always known what family meant. I've seen how she's been willing to give up anything for hers. She'll do the same thing for Katie. She's already given the baby her heart…the rest will just be a bonus. Katie will have a mother and father, and maybe someday soon, siblings. A house full of love. That's what I'm giving her."

Mia realized she wanted that for Katie. She loved her enough to give her up to that sort of dream. "Yes. You're right, they sound perfect. When will she be leaving?"

"She won't."

"I don't understand. You said—"

"I said I found her the perfect family. I did." He reached into his jacket pocket, and opened a box. "I'll buy you a diamond, or whatever else you want, but this is the ring I wanted to give you when I asked you to marry me. Katie and I picked it up yesterday after we left your house."

"Mac?" Mia said weakly.

"It's like Mrs. Z's. Even with her Italian last name, she's Irish at heart. She told me the story of the Celtic Knot. The legend says it represents the interweaving of two lives. In our case, it's not just two, it's three. I love you. I'd love you—I'd be asking you to marry me—even if we'd never found Katie."

She gave him a look and he laughed. "Okay, so maybe it would have taken me longer to realize it. But we did find her, and I do realize it. I love you. We're a family. It's meant to be. You and me…we're meant to be."

"Are you sure? You said—"

"I said a lot of things, but I never said the words *I love you* before to any woman. I never thought I would. But then I never thought I'd be a father either, and have discovered that's just what I am. I'm Katie's father. She's mine. She's a part of me. A part of you. Like this ring, we're linked. Tangled up in each other. And I don't want to try to untangle us."

"Me either," she said, throwing her arms around his neck and, with Katie gurgling happily between them, she kissed him. "Yes. You're the rest of my dream. A dream I wasn't sure would come true."

"Yes?"

"Yes, I'll marry you. I want to be your wife, I want to be Katie's mother."

"About school?"

"I'll go back. Maybe start taking one course a term this fall."

"It will take a while for you to finish that way."

"I want to be home with the kids. When they're small. When they're older, I'll have finished and will look for a job."

"Kids?" he asked weakly.

"Kids. At least two or three more. You'll need a basketball hoop in the drive, like the Zumigalas have. And you'll need to meet my brothers. They'll act tough at first, they like to think they're protecting me, but they'll love you. They're family. And—"

"Mia, all this is fine," he said softly, his index finger running lightly along her jawline, "but right now, you need to shut up and kiss me."

"I'd love to Larry." And with Katie caught up between them, they kissed and sealed their promise.

At that moment, the three of them were truly what they were always meant to be…a family.

Epilogue

"Katie O'Keefe Mackenzie, you stop right there," Mia insisted.

She bounced Merry on her hip as she chased after Katie, aka hell on-wheels.

"You know better than to ride your bike so close to the street. You scared me."

"Sorry, Mama," she said with a whisper. She jumped off the bike and hugged Mia and Merry both, just as Mac's car pulled into the driveway.

"Daddy," Katie screamed.

"How's my girl?" he asked as he scooped her up and dodged the lawn full of toys as he walked toward Mia.

"Good, Daddy, only I can't ride my bike near the street."

"Right you are," he said. He turned to Mia. There was a look in his eye that always took her breath away.

"How was my Merry Maid Marion today?" he asked softly.

She stroked the hair of their new daughter, Marion O'Keefe's namesake. "Sweet as always."

"I'm not sweet, Daddy," Katie said. She flexed her muscles. "I'm tough."

"You're tough all right." He kissed Katie's head, then smiled at Mia. "Mom and Dad called my cell. They'll be here in about half an hour."

"Nana and Papa. How long's half an hour?" Katie cried.

"Not long at all," Mac said with a laugh. "Uncle Chet, Uncle Marty and Uncle Ryan are coming to dinner, too."

"I love family day," Katie said. "I'll blow out the candles and get some presents and then…"

Mia listened to Katie prattle about her plans for the celebration. It was her anniversary with Mac. Two years ago today they'd married and adopted Katie legally.

"An amazing time," Mac said, looking at his family. "Just the first of many."

Mia looked at Mac and Katie as she clutched Merry a little tighter.

Her family.

A family built on the most important thing of all…love.

* * * * *

Rediscover the remarkable O'Hurley family...

#1 *New York Times* bestselling author

NORA ROBERTS

BORN O'HURLEY

Starring her mesmerizing family of Irish performers in America.

The unique upbringing of the O'Hurley triplet sisters
and their mysterious older brother has led to four
extraordinary lives. This collector's-size edition
showcases the stories of Abby and Maddy O'Hurley.

Available in August 2004.

Where love comes alive™

SILHOUETTE *Romance*®

Coming September 2004 from

KAREN ROSE SMITH

Once Upon a Baby...

(Silhouette Romance #1737)

Marriage was the last thing on eternal bachelor Simon Blackstone's mind when he offered to help the very beautiful—and very pregnant—Risa Parker. But the closer Simon gets to the glowing mother-to-be, the closer he'll come to wanting to claim Risa and her baby as his own....

Available at your favorite retail outlet.